***

A tarnished subcaptain, a repair technician with a past, and two genetically engineered cats must join forces to save an important factory.

*Military Subcaptain **Kedron Tauceti** counts the days until he can leave the rare metals factory and his current duty station as the liaison to the galactic government's Criminal Restitution and Indenture Obligation system. He's more than ready to get his career back on track on a new base, even if it means leaving behind the one person who makes him want to stay. Not that he's told her, because technically, he's her warden.*

*Former financial specialist and current repair tech **Ferra Barray**, hiding from her past, only has three months to go on her restitution sentence. Unfortunately, the local shark behind every illegal scheme in the facility wants her to steal for him, and she's running out of excuses. And now the heroically handsome Tauceti, who she hoped could help, is transferring out.*

Everything changes when Ferra discovers two genetically modified cats. Saving them takes incredible risks. She doesn't know what she'll do if she can't convince Tauceti to rescue the cats and keep them until she's free to come for them.

But when trouble erupts at the factory, it might just be the cats who save them.

ALSO BY CAROL VAN NATTA

Space Opera - Central Galactic Concordance Series

- Last Ship Off Polaris-G (Novella)
- Overload Flux (Book 1)
- Minder Rising (Book 2)
- Zero Flux (Novella)
- Pico's Crush (Book 3)
- Pet Trade (Novella)
- Jumper's Hope (Book 4)
- Cats of War (Novella)
- Galactic Search and Rescue (Novella)
- Escape from Nova Nine (Novella)
- Spark Transform (Book 5)

Retro Science Fiction Comedy

- Hooray for Holopticon

Paranormal Romance

- Shifter Mate Magic (Ice Age Shifters #1)
- Shift of Destiny (Ice Age Shifters #2)
- Heart of a Dire Wolf (Ice Age Shifters #3)
- Dire Wolf Wanted (Ice Age Shifters #4)
- Shifter's Storm (Ice Age Shifters #5)
- In Graves Below (Magic, New Mexico)

CATS OF WAR

A CENTRAL GALACTIC CONCORDANCE
NOVELLA

CAROL VAN NATTA

CHAVANCH
PRESS

1

High Command Ground Division Subcaptain Kedron Tauceti longed to open the window in his office just once before leaving.

Not that he wanted more insects in everything, but even fresh air that smelled like a swamp would alleviate his office's stuffiness. The Central Galactic Concordance government section of the building that housed him, the CRIO staff, and the lone Citizen Protection Service representative was a later addition to the metals filtering and processing facility. The retrofit ducting did little to improve the inadequate ventilation and air handling. He'd been through three portable fans in his two-year tour of duty, and the fourth died an hour ago.

At least he wouldn't have to put up with the upcoming sweltering summer heat. He'd be on his way to his new post in four ten-days, six single days, and twenty hours. He didn't even pretend he hadn't started a countdown clock.

Serving as second-in-command for the small military

base on Merganukhan, a backwater planet if ever there was one, probably wasn't most people's idea of a plum assignment. Unless their previous stint was the military liaison to the CGC's Criminal Restitution and Indenture Obligation system at a rare metals processing facility in the middle of a gigantic, insect-ridden, moss-laden swamp.

His current, soon-to-be-former, assignment was partly protection and partly punishment. He'd expected consequences from exposing a theft ring, because it tarnished the name of a military family as fabled as his own. From almost his first day as logistics chief on the huge, multi-divisional military base on Parlayan Six, Commodore Salah Chuma M'tendere had singled him out for much more than professional attention.

He hadn't known her long enough to be interested in a personal relationship, much less intimacy. When he'd figured out the real attraction had been his access to physical storage and quartermaster systems to enable sophisticated thievery, he'd gathered evidence and given it to High Command.

Unfortunately, the fallout made the entire chain of command look incompetent and lazy. That was only partly true, because the theft ring had been as clever as they were bold. Only complacency and rising greed got them caught. Most of them, anyway.

He wondered if the military investigators ever found the rumored treasure ship that M'Tendere reportedly hid before her high-profile court-martial at headquarters on Concordance Prime. By that time, High Command had appointed him to the CRIO post on Olaza Okomvelo "for his safety," instead of subcaptain of a mech division, for which he'd trained and positioned himself. His stint at the Argint d'Apa plant had put him out of sight—and conveniently unavailable to journalists—for the last two years.

He fervently hoped the long-awaited reassignment notice meant High Command had finally forgiven him for his good deed. It would take a decade to get his career back on track.

The clock display of his wallcomp declared the time to be midday, but the farking thing was only right for about an hour after a manual reset. The military-issue percomp on his wrist said it was actually close to the start of evening meal service, and his stomach agreed. Once the technology repair specialist came by, he'd be free to go eat, meet with the security chief, and take his customary evening walk before hitting the military gym.

He'd considered canceling the tech appointment, since he'd be gone soon, but he'd kept it on principle. He'd been submitting unanswered trouble reports for two years. The overworked and chronically understaffed facility's tech repair lab was finally getting around to checking out all his perennially malfunctioning office systems. At least he could leave everything in working order for his successor.

Kedron knew he shouldn't complain. The local CRIO installation was well run and passed audits with all green flags. He'd heard horror stories from the CRIO staff about notorious hellhole installations and rumors of secret installations that were even worse. It would have been just his luck to be assigned to one of those.

At Argint d'Apa, military veterans were few and far between, so the liaison job left him with a great deal of free time. The murky local chain of command meant few orders and little oversight from above. He submitted status reports and assessments for military indenturees, studied and took online training courses in things that interested him and might further his career, and kept himself in shape by visiting the gym a lot. He had yet to convince himself he'd been doing important work for High Command or the galactic government.

The biggest local issue he'd seen was the facility's chronic and currently resurgent problem with recreational chems. They were forbidden for all indenturees, but not for staff. When he'd asked about the policy or reported potential trouble, the facility manager had firmly and repeatedly told him to mind his own jurisdiction.

The other reason he didn't cancel the repair appointment was the technician who'd made the appointment, Indenturee Ferra Barray. In a facility full of restive, resentful, or resigned people—including him, sometimes—her cheery demeanor and lively sense of humor were a breath of fresh air.

He would've had no occasion to interact with her at all, except her records mistakenly identified her as ex-military, so he'd conducted her intake orientation four months ago. The regular CRIO staff was short-handed and overworked, so he'd kept Barray on his assignment list.

He'd had regular check-ins and several more random interactions with her since, including being stuck for a day in a shelter lockdown for a hurricane event. She'd made friends with everyone and kept the nervous indenturees occupied by teaching them an elaborate, convoluted logic game that Kedron was half-convinced she'd invented on the spot.

He secretly wanted to get to know her better, and maybe become friends. That, however, was a no-go, full-warn, all-red stop. He refused to go within a thousand kilometers of striking up a personal relationship with an indenturee. Thanks to his last post, he knew exactly what coercion felt like. How the pressure left a sick, sour stomach and constant anxiety.

He would rather let himself be savaged by the big hellhound escapee-retriever dogs that the plant security guards kept than do that to someone else. Bored guards sometimes caught unlucky wild animals and threw them to the dogs for "training," which also happened to involve betting. Kedron hated that he couldn't stop them. The only thing he or the CRIO staff could do was make sure it stayed on the civilian side of the compound.

Right on time, Barray knocked on the sliding door frame, then entered. She carried a bag slung over her shoulder. "Greetings, Subcaptain."

"Indenturee Barray." He nodded. "Thank you for coming."

She looked around and smiled when she saw the clock display. "Wallcomp troubles?"

Disgruntlement drove him to his feet. "*Everything* troubles. The only reliable tech in here is my percomp." He raised his arm to show the military gauntlet. "The wallcomp, the deskcomp, the light and enviro controls, the door lock, you name it, they're all glitchy." He pointed his chin toward the dead fan. "Even that sparked out an hour ago."

Her eyebrow raised. "And you're just reporting all this now?"

"What do you mean, now?" He took a deep breath to control his temper. "I have been submitting trouble reports for the last two years."

"That's odd." Skepticism crossed her face. "The records show two complaints from two years ago, a replacement fan a year ago, then nothing else until yesterday." She unfolded a battered tablet and brought up a holo display that showed four entries.

"Nonsense." He reached for his deskcomp, hesitated, then used his own percomp instead. It only took a moment to find and display the twenty-seven complaints. "These are what I submitted." He was glad he'd thought to keep copies.

"That's, uh, quite a list." She held out her plant-issued tablet. "Can you send those to me? I'll check when I get back to the repair lab."

He found the tablet's signal and transferred the list. "Done."

She put the tablet in her thigh pocket and looked around again. "Let's try for a quick win and fix the door lock first. That's security and safety, so it has priority." She took a tech scanner and a multitool out of her bag and turned to the door.

Rather than be a nuisance, he made himself sit and bring up the deskcomp display, so she wouldn't feel scrutinized. Her running commentary as she removed the panel amused him.

"Oh, no, I won't hurt you. Just a little probe." She pulled a datawire out of her bag and inserted it into the exposed connector. "There's a good module. Tell me all your troubles."

"Do you always talk to tech?" he asked.

"I talk to everything." She chuckled. "Blame my childhood on a space station. We couldn't afford pets." She turned to him. "I'll keep it in my head."

He raised his eyebrows. "You have a tech skulljack?" He resisted the impulse to touch his, hidden behind his ear. It had been quiet for two years, but soon, it would again enable him to interface with the AI of an assault tank or a three-story-tall military spider mech.

Laughter bubbled up out of her. "No, I meant I'll be quiet." She shook her head. "Even if I did have one, CRIO would have forcibly flatlined it. Thank chaos I flunked the minder tests, or the Citizen Protection Service would have put me on disruptor drugs, too." Her mouth twisted in scorn. "I guess CRIO and the CPS think all indentures are threats to the galactic peace."

He agreed with her acerbic contempt, but it wasn't politic to say so. He shrugged a shoulder. "You don't have to be quiet for my sake." He pointed to his display filled with flat photos and holos. "I'm just familiarizing myself with the native flora and fauna near my new post."

"Oh? Where is it?" She frowned. "Or is that crypto?"

"It's not secret at all. I'll be second-in-command of the combined military base on Merganukhan."

She chuckled. "Gotta be a Fourth Wave terraform. All the good member planet names were taken by then."

Her humor was infectious. "Third Wave, but the name is made up. When the colonists finally paid off the settlement company debt, the CGC High Council wouldn't let them rename the planet to 'Suck Flux, RSI.'"

Laughter burst out of her. "Too bad. I'd go out of my way to visit a planet with that name." She waved fingers in a sketch of a military salute. "Congratulations on the new post, Subcaptain, and good luck." She turned back to the door lock.

He knew others found him to be too focused and intense, which is why he had few friends. Being shy and slow to open up didn't help. He'd tried to change that in his liaison position but hadn't gotten very far. He lived on the compound and disliked most of the guards. He had little in common with the CRIO staff or the regular company employees. He preferred to avoid the CPS representative, and was an ocean away from the planet's only military base.

It was a sad commentary on his life that the only person in the facility to wish him well was an indenturee repaying a hefty restitution debt for destruction of CGC military property.

Ferra's day had started badly, then gone downhill and off a cliff from there.

Once again, dreams of flitter crashes and hunting for something lost, with two voices calling her, woke her more than once. She was short on sleep and long on clumsiness.

She'd flatlined the controls in the plant manager's expensive solardry unit. She'd barely escaped being cornered in the indenturee recreation hall by one of Lambru's recruiters. After the midday meal, a guard stopped and scanned her for contraband, all because she'd been carrying an empty crate. The same guard who passively watched her carrying crates full of equipment through that same central hallway every day.

She'd been looking forward to spending a few minutes with Subcaptain Tauceti. He was the only person in the entire facility who treated her with respect.

All right, that wasn't quite fair. The repair lab supervisor appreciated that she'd reduced his backlog of tech service requests, but to him, she was a replaceable commodity. The guards weren't outright abusive, but they were bored enough to let trouble among the indenturees play out for the entertainment value, as long as it didn't affect the regular staff or impact plant productivity. The less said about the guards who handled the dogs, the better.

Most of the indenturees kept to themselves and tracked their restitution balances like they were winning lottery numbers. The few that perpetrated inside scams and schemes were a pain in the ass and definitely to be avoided.

Tauceti had been her hidden ace, the one person she hoped she could go to if, despite her precautions, bad trouble found her. And now he was leaving. Frellin' hell.

The door lock was an easy fix, once she removed the underpowered spinwire scaffold some previous tech had made instead of simply replacing the failed C6 dot. Experience had taught her to carry several in her bag. She was careful not to disturb the security connectors. None of her business that the company monitored the High Command military liaison's office door.

She tested the wall control several times, then turned to face him. "The door should work now. Try it from your desk."

He touched the controls. The door obligingly opened, closed, or locked each time. He smiled. "Yes, thank you."

She stepped over to the wallcomp. "Yeah, I see you, looking all innocent."

He chuckled. "Sly troublemakers, are they?"

She nodded. "Oh, yeah. Either that, or they have swamp allergies, like us humans."

"Mold or spores, perhaps. The scientists complain about them." He glanced at his percomp, then went back to reading. A faint rumble came from the direction of his stomach.

He was probably hungry. It likely took a lot of concentrated protein and nutrients to keep his muscular body in such great condition. He made even the boring daily uniform look heroic. With his strong jaw and piercing blue eyes, he belonged in military recruiting holos. The bold geometric designs cut into the sides of his short brown hair offset his reserved demeanor, giving him an air of danger.

Dangerous to her, anyway. Apparently, being tired and cranky made her vulnerable to nova-hot men. She would never have acted on her secret fantasy of pouncing on him, because it would have ruined their relationship and compromised them both. Besides, he seemed completely oblivious to even blatant sexual flirtation from women or men, at least from what she'd seen.

Perhaps he needed an emotional connection with someone before becoming interested in getting physical. In which case, it was just as well he was leaving, before their friendly professional relationship had a chance to grow into anything personal. Loneliness made people do stupid things.

The wallcomp's small access door refused to open. She tried to pop off its decorative faceplate, but it clung to the bezel for dear life. When she finally pried it off, it slipped out of her fingers and landed on top of her foot, then bounced on the floor. "Ow!" She picked it up. "Sorry."

"Are you all right?" His concern seemed genuine.

"Fine." She fought off a blush. "I'm a certified non-adept. If this is the worst that happens, it'll be a good day." She gave him a self-deprecating smile. "Swamp allergies are giving me weird flying dreams and waking me up, so I'm sleep-deprived, too. I've got a medic appointment in the morning." And she was babbling to the pretty man. She gave herself a mental shake as she leaned the faceplate against the wall. "If it's okay with you, I'll assess all your tech now, then come back with the right parts."

He nodded. "As of now, my schedule is clear for the next ten-day."

His expression said he didn't know how he felt about that. He was a decent man with a sense of humor hiding under his contained personality. She'd felt bad about lying to him during the intake interview, because he seemed like an ethical man, too.

Oh, stop, she ordered herself.

Tauceti probably fluxed her drives because she missed her ordinary life, when she'd had friends, and one or two more-than-friends for physical affection and comfort. That was before everything blew up, thanks to her no-good, dead-to-her, may-he-slowly-rot-in-transit-space twin brother.

Those thoughts were a deeply-rutted, rocky path. "Move on, Barray," she muttered to herself. She picked up the scanner and focused on the wallcomp.

Twenty minutes later had her wishing she'd taken a

backbreaking processing plant job instead of demonstrating a little tech experience during the skills assessment for restitution job placement.

Every single tech device in Tauceti's office, from his wallcomp, to his clock display, to his frelling portable fan, was infested with surveillance tech. Redundant, overlapping, interfering surveillance tech, some of which had been installed by rank amateurs.

Telling him would reveal her expertise, which was far deeper than her official records hinted at. She should know, because she'd written them herself. Deactivating the tech would bring the same result.

Also, if she'd misread Tauceti, and he deserved to be that tightly monitored, taking any action would expose the investigation.

Despite what the crime and conviction record said that had gotten her to Argint d'Apa, she was not anti-social. She'd been keeping a low profile for safety and working off her self-imposed sentence for being mind-bogglingly trusting and desperately stupid.

She needed more information on Tauceti before she could decide what to do. Her job meant she'd been in enough of the Argint d'Apa systems to know she could do some investigating of her own and not get caught. Her former specialty had been multi-node fractal meshes for financial systems, not processing plants that collected rare metals from the runoff that filtered through the swamp, but they had remarkably similar principles.

In the meantime, the people at the other end of the surveillance feed might find it suspicious if she didn't at least make a token attempt at her job. "Could I borrow your guest chair again? I've got time to fix your clock before I go."

"Of course." He watched as she carried it over and stepped up onto it, then went back to his deskcomp display.

Knowing the various spy eyes were watching, she fumbled around in the clock systems, as if improvising. Which she would have been, when she first arrived. Luckily, she knew how to read schematics and she'd learned quickly. Once she paid her debt, she'd need a new career, but it wouldn't be a repair tech. Her experience in Argint d'Apa proved they only saw grumpy people.

Surreptitiously, she overpowered her multi-tool, then touched it to the offending, power-grabbing module that contained a spy eye and who knew what else. She jumped when it actually sparked. *Frelling amateurs.* "Sorry, little clock."

"Are you okay?" he asked.

"Fine." She isolated the fried module but left it in place. "Just a bad connector." She traced the other connectors to make sure no other vampire tech was stealing power. "I think I've got it fixed."

She stepped off the chair and carried it back to its place.

Just as she picked up the handles to her bag, his office door opened to admit a knee-high cleaning bot. It raced into the room, zoomed by her feet, and banged itself into the south wall. It backed up and did it twice more.

On the third run, Ferra intercepted it. "Come here, you." She grunted as she lifted the heavy bot and turned it on its side. Tri-treads spun in place, like a turtle trying to right itself. She opened the concealed access plate and used the handle of her multitool to kill the power. "Does this happen to you a lot?"

"Are you talking to the bot or me?" Tauceti was suddenly close and looking down at her.

She covered her surprise with a laugh. "Both. You go first."

"No. Bots don't usually go berserk in my office." A twinkle in his eye belied his serious expression.

"Wonder why it's out in daytime." She patted its shell. "If it's still here when I come back tomorrow, I'll find out—"

"What are you doing to that bot?"

A woman stood in the doorway, arms crossed. Her digital name tag proclaimed her to be E. Calderosh, Facility Maintenance, and tailored work clothes confirmed her to be regular staff, not an indenturee. She looked mid-thirties, but could have been five times that old if she'd had regular maintenance or a full-body makeover. A crown of frizzy gold and silver braids kept her hair in place. Her expression made Ferra feel like a teenage miscreant.

"The bot malfunctioned," said Tauceti firmly. "Barray turned it off."

Calderosh's suspicious look cleared. "Oh, well, that's all right, then. I'll take it." She left for a moment, then came back in the room with a gravcart that had the sorry remains of another cleaning bot on it. She looked at Tauceti. "You haven't seen any other bots, have you? Some of these big ones and a bunch of the smaller ones are missing." She shaped her hands as if to hold something the size of a sports ball.

He shook his head. "No." Even standing casually, he looked like a vid star. No wrinkles, no dust, not a hair out of place.

Ferra stood and moved away from the bot, only to stumble over her own equipment bag and land on her ass. Her multitool went flying and bounced off the bot, then off Tauceti's shin.

"Sorry." She picked herself and the multitool up off the floor. She hid her embarrassment by bending over to seal and pick up her bag, allowing her loose, wavy hair to hide her face.

Clearly, she was a menace. For safety, she sould go straight to her room and stay there until the bad-luck chaos cloud moved on, except she still had things to do.

He glanced at her. "No harm done."

"At least the damn dogs didn't try to eat this one." Calderosh lifted the bot onto the cart with ease. "I have a feeling some of the bots got past the outer fence and are trying to clean the swamp." She rolled her eyes. "My boss will probably want me to go out and retrieve them."

Ferra laughed. "Because they'll smell so good when you get them back."

"Exactly," said Calderosh. "If you find any, turn them in. The plant manager posted a restitution bounty for them."

Surprised at the woman's friendliness, Ferra smiled. "Good to know."

Tauceti raised an eyebrow. "Has anyone tried turning the same one in multiple times?"

Calderosh chuckled. "A few of usual chiselers tried, but I hid asset tracers in the returned bots."

A lock of hair fell in Ferra's face. When she went to brush it back, the pass-tracker cuff on her wrist suddenly fell off and bounced on the floor in two pieces. She must have hit it when she fell. She scooped up the two pieces with a sigh. Her supervisor would probably charge her for printing a new one, since it would be her third.

Calderosh dug into one of the bellows pockets in her vest. "Here. Glue it with this until you can get it fixed." She produced a tube and held it out with a smile. "Locktight water sealer. Handiest stuff on the base."

Ferra shook her head. "Sorry, I don't know how to use it."

Calderosh pointed to the blue end. "Put the paste on the broken ends, hold them together, then zap it with the microcharger on the top. Hardens in seconds."

The bracelet-style percomp around Calderosh's wrist began blinking. She touched her earwire and subvocalized. As she listened, her expression transitioned into annoyance.

She blew out a noisy breath and grabbed the gravcart's control bar. "An indenturee named Healey sabotaged the kennel doors before her unauthorized departure, so of course, I'm the only non-indenturee in the whole facility who can let the damn hellhounds out." She handed the tube to Ferra. "Leave it with the subcaptain when you're done."

Calderosh stomped out with the gravcart trailing her like a child's wagon.

Ferra looked at the tube, then put it on Tauceti's

desk. "I'll leave this with you right now. Considering the day I'm having, I'd probably seal my fingers together."

His expression softened as he glanced at the broken pieces in her hand. "Want me to try?"

"Sure." She put them on the desk, then backed away. "I'll just stand over here, in case clumsiness is communicable."

He deftly applied dabs of paste on each broken piece. "You're not clumsy." Pushing the ends together right the first time, he held the cuff together with one hand and touched the microcharger tip to the joins. "You're just tired." He leaned over his desk to examine the joins under the bright lamp.

"Yeah, that too." A violent, wet sneeze took her by surprise. She barely had time to cover her face with her elbow. "And allergic."

Good thing she wasn't trying to impress Tauceti, because otherwise, she'd be thoroughly mortified by the whole visit and have to avoid him for at least a ten-day.

"The medics have chems for that." He handed her the repaired pass-tracker.

Ferra laughed. "I'm pretty sure no chems in the galaxy will cure clumsiness." She slipped the tracker onto her wrist. "Besides, I avoid any drugs if at all possible. If there's an obscure side-effect that's worse than the disease, I'm guaranteed to get it." She hitched the bag's strap higher on her shoulder. "I'll get out of your orbit so you can go eat."

He nodded and glanced at his percomp. "What time will you be here tomorrow?"

"Assuming no front-office emergencies, nine-hundred-ish. Maybe earlier if the medic clears me fast."

"I'll be here." He went back behind his desk. "Get some rest."

She felt like she ought to salute or yes-sir him, even though she wasn't military. "Uh, thanks for fixing my cuff."

"No problem." He sat and turned on his deskcomp display.

For a moment, she thought he looked lonely, sitting in his perfect uniform, in his perfect office that had nothing personal to relieve the generic sterility.

She shook her head as she left his office. *Move on, Barray.*

3

Kedron had unexpected free time after his quick cafeteria dinner. Argint d'Apa's security chief had canceled their regular meeting, likely because the guards hadn't yet recaptured Healey, even after deploying the genetically modified hellhounds. The shady pet trade had originally designed them as status symbols for the wealthy; the military found them useful and expropriated the patents. Argint d'Apa security got them as part of their deal with CRIO. The dense biomass of the swamp and the types of metals in the mountain runoff water made ordinary tracers and trackers next to worthless outside the plant compound's perimeter.

While Kedron wouldn't miss the Argint d'Apa facility, he would miss the swamp. He'd disliked it at first, the same way most staffers still did, but it had grown on him. He'd spent time studying its ecology and gone with the biodiversity scientists on a few sample-collection expeditions. Living so close to untamed nature made it easier to understand how everything, from the majestic giant trees to annoying clouds of gnats, had a place. Maybe he did, too, even if he couldn't see it.

He put away his uniform and decided to walk laps on the campus's wide perimeter walkway, rather than spend another evening alone in the gym. Regulations restricted it to military personnel, and he'd never seen the CPS representative use it.

As much as possible, he kept his interactions with her in virtual space. As a mid-level telepath, she could read thoughts, and as a low-level sifter, she could affect brain chemicals, detect lies, and sense the use of active minder talents. Military personnel caught with minder talents earned an immediate, permanent transfer to the CPS's Minder Corps.

Kedron's minder talent wasn't much, just an ability to use seemingly unrelated information to find things of interest, but he'd rather direct traffic for a city of half a billion or be an indenturee than work for the Minder Corps. Too many private family stories warned of how badly the Minder Corps treated its personnel. He'd learned to hide his talent well enough to beat the CPS Testing Center for mandatory age twelve and seventeen tests, and random ones since, but some sifters were better than the testing equipment. Fortunately, minder talents in the patterner class were hard for even high-level sifters to detect.

He pulled on pants and a specially treated long-sleeved top to ward off biting insects. Last, he stepped into one of his few indulgences—custom-tailored, waterproof, adaptive boots. Even with myriad modern transportation options, Ground Div gunnin, from the lowest ranker to High Command commodores, spent a lot of time walking, running, and marching. Good boots made all the difference.

He looked out the north-facing window of his quarters to check the weather and the path. Non-essential indenturees were on lockdown, and half the staff was busy, so he wasn't surprised to see it deserted. The tall perimeter fence's horizontal power lines beyond the road-glass pathway glowed faintly as reminders of their presence. The overhead and glass path lights blinked on and off erratically, then stayed off. Twilight and mold sometimes messed with the sensors.

Shadowed movement caught his eye. Someone carrying a shallow, rectangular crate stepped off the path toward the exterior powered fence. The figure knelt right in front of the fence and set the crate down. After furtive looks left and right, the hunched figure slid something under the fence.

Instead of zapping the person into insensibility or setting off the alarm, the visible bottom three fence lines between the two posts raised like a curtain, leaving a torso-height gap. The figure quickly extended a pole to push the crate outside the fence as far as possible, until it butted up against the big rock outcropping. He or she retracted the pole and picked up the device from the dirt. The fence line sank and straightened to its usual position.

The lights flickered on briefly. The figure pulled on a hood and hunched forward, but he'd already recognized the face. Ferra Barray.

She stepped onto the path and headed west. The

lights came on and stayed bright. He watched until she vanished.

Protocol said to report anything unusual to the security chief, but Kedron had repeatedly been told, politely but sternly, to stick to his own star lane.

He wished he could come up with a more probable theory than suspecting that Barray was dealing contraband. A non-indenturee confederate would likely pick up the goods. Chems, pilfered equipment or tech, and stolen raw metals were all likely candidates.

He wouldn't have tagged her for a thief. She'd been convicted of crashing a friend's air-racing yacht into a Central Galactic Concordance government launch hangar that housed military orbiters. When she couldn't pay the court-ordered restitution, the CGC arbiter remanded her to the CRIO system. The record implied she'd been chemmed to the gills.

That didn't sync with her comment earlier that day about avoiding drugs of any sort, but everyone did stupid things now and again.

He wanted Barray to be the person he thought she was, but his experience with the theft ring situation taught him not to be swayed by what he wished to be true, and to look at the actual facts. He needed to know what was in the crate.

Crossing to his closet, he pulled out a dark jacket and wrist lights, plus a bigger floating light.

On the way to the facility's main ground gate on the other side of the complex, he tried to think of a reason to be trudging around in the swamp after dark. He was a lousy liar, so it had to be plausible. The best he could come up with was that he'd seen a potential problem with the perimeter fence but wanted to confirm it before reporting it.

The gate guards checked his credential and biometric, then waved him on through without so much as a curious glance.

He saw no one on the inside lighted walkway as he made his way carefully around the outside from the south. The compacted dirt had deteriorated into mud holes in some spots but was mostly intact. The glass-over-rock base would protect the facility for a while, but he had no doubt the swamp would eventually win, if left unchecked.

Chilly water soaked the bottom half of his pants by the time he found the crate. He crouched beside it and checked his surroundings, then turned on his lights to examine it for traps or trouble. Finally, he opened the lid.

Inside, a mother muskrat and three tiny, furry brown babies nestled in a bed of wilting water vines and rusting lettuce leaves.

Relief flooded him as he quickly closed the lid. Ferra wasn't dealing, she was rescuing. He'd once accidentally discovered her vomiting after seeing the guards throw a stray animal to the hellhounds. He'd brought her towels and a water pouch and felt guilty because all he could do was help her clean up the mess.

Since he was already muddy, he carried the crate farther into the swamp. He set it on a hillock near the water. The young muskrat had bred very early in the season, so her babies might not survive anyway, but at least now they'd have a fighting chance.

He opened the lid and encouraged the little family to get out. The mother squealed in evident distress. He hated to take the crate, but its garish yellow color and plant logo would attract attention if a patrolling guard saw it. He left the bedding and the lettuce on the hillock, then collapsed the crate flat and carried it back.

Once again, the guards asked no questions, just pointed him to the cleaning jets and solardry so he wouldn't track muddy footprints through the halls.

By the time he stepped into the hot shower in his private fresher, his satisfaction at discovering the benevolent nature of Ferra's secret had morphed into curiosity about a new mystery. How had she breached the fence?

4

Ferra's bone-deep exhaustion made her wonder if she wasn't actually just dreaming about waiting her turn to pay in the slow-moving cafeteria line.

After finishing her shift, eating late, and sneaking the young mother muskrat and her babies out of the compound, Ferra had gone straight to bed.

Unfortunately, the dreams were more vivid than ever, with two distinct thought patterns in her head. One was lonely and worried, and the other was in pain and cried for help. It didn't take a certified therapy telepath to figure out her subconscious was manifesting her fears the only way it knew how. If the medics couldn't counter the allergen affecting her, maybe they'd give her a dormo patch. Seven uninterrupted hours of sleep would be worth losing bonus money for being on call after-hours.

She pushed her tray forward in the track, debating on splurging on fresh sweetfruit and caffeine to supplement her usual cheap mealpack and water pouch. No such thing as a free breakfast for indenturees.

A hissed argument and commotion behind her made her and everyone else turn to look.

Too late, she realized it was a setup. Indenturee Lambru cut in line in front of her with his tray full of expensive, freshly made hot dishes and premium real coffee. She'd trained herself to track and avoid his various confederates, who she thought of as remora, but in her fog of exhaustion, she'd forgotten to track the head shark himself.

He might be wearing the same indenturee uniform as everyone else, but the details painted the image of an intersex who presented male and had a taste for stylish shoes, resilk undershirts, and pearlescent cosmetics.

His mild and meek air belied his involvement with every illegal activity in Argint d'Apa, both indenturee and staff. His official story was that he'd been a low-level employee for a pharma blackmarketer. However, his current restitution debt was an order of magnitude higher than hers, despite five years in the CRIO system. Luckily, a departing indenturee had warned her early on, or she might have been unwittingly reeled into his schemes.

He gave her a pleasant smile. "Hello, Barray."

She nodded, allowing her eyelids to droop a little, as if barely functional and pre-verbal. Not far from the truth, actually.

His expression transitioned into almost shy diffidence. "I wonder if I might ask a favor?"

She gave him credit for his acting ability and for getting straight to the point. Ever since her first month in the tech department, his intermediaries had been looking for a lever to get to her. Thanks to having had to bail her brother out of trouble dozens of times, she knew the type, and knew how to play dumb or avoid them.

She yawned to cover her glance toward the guard who was chatting up one of the food servers. No help there.

Lambru smiled as he pushed his tray forward. "Up too early, or up too late?"

She shrugged. No one moved into the gap in line behind her, so no help there, either.

He pushed his tray forward, then grabbed hers and pulled it next to his fast enough to make its contents slide to the edge. "I'm so sorry." He lifted the meal pack and pouch with exaggerated care and returned them to the center of her tray.

She wasn't surprised to see her tray now sported a hand-printed list peeking out from under the mealpack. Indenturees weren't allowed personal percomps or unmonitored net access, forcing them back to the pre-flight Stone Age for communications.

She knew how this went. If she accepted the list, she was on the hook. If she tore up the list or reported it, he'd make an example of her. Delay was her only option. She shoved her hands in her vest pockets and looked up, then back to him.

His oily smile smacked of used flitter sales. "I'm sure we can come to a trade arrangement that benefits everyone." His tone took on an unctuous quality. "You will find it very worth your..." He trailed off with a frown and a sniff. "Is something burning?"

She waited until he noticed her mealpack's heater had set the whole pack on fire.

"Shit," she said loudly. She pulled the water pouch off the tray, then fumbled to open it.

The paper list under the mealpack caught fire and emitted dark smoke.

She grunted with effort. Just as she got the pouch open, the overhead fire suppression system opened up and doused the fire, plus everything in a four-meter radius, with orange foam.

Indenturees sputtered in dismay and outrage. Lambru backed up. He lost his footing and cracked his elbow hard on a nearby chair.

A food server and two guards converged on their position, with more on the way.

Between the acrid smell of the burned tray, the carbonized smell of burned food, and the cloying citrus scent in the foam, Ferra's stomach threatened revolt.

"What happened?" demanded a guard.

Ferra pointed to the mess on the tray. "Mealpack heater overload."

The suppression foam made a soupy gelatin on the hot tray. Everywhere else, it turned to powder, causing several people to sneeze.

"Third fail this month," groused the food server. His thick Islander accent gave a musical cadence to his words. He opened a yellow collapsible crate to collect the mess.

A guard peered at Ferra. "You look pale."

"I just need something to eat." She pointed her chin toward the blackened tray. "Preferably not overcooked."

The food server chuckled. "I bring you one different.

No charge." He raised his voice and addressed the rest of the people with ruined food. "If you no pay, go back to kitchen. They fix again." He repeated it in Mandarin, which was better than his English.

Ferra sipped water from the pouch she was still holding. Her stomach gurgled.

"What if we already paid?" whined an indenturee.

The food server pointed to the woman just striding in from the office area. "Ask manager."

Ferra stayed with the guards when the affected indenturees headed toward the kitchen. Lambru's irritated expression could have been for her or the mess, but he followed the others.

She stood quietly aside while the guard subvocalized a quick report to the shift supervisor. The food server brought her a new mealpack with a different logo on it. She nodded her thanks, then turned to the guard.

"Permission to take this with me for later?" She brushed orange powder off the front of her and didn't want to think about what her hair looked like. "I have a medic appointment in fifteen minutes, and a CPS re-test after that."

The guard shrugged. "Yeah, go ahead. Just don't leave it for the swamp rats or the birds to find."

Ferra ducked out the cafeteria's side door and made a quick stop in her cell to stash the mealpack. She knew from experience that anything but water and maybe a little bread would make her nausea worse.

At the clinic, the medic's blood tests said no allergies, toxins, molds, or weird spores. She'd described her dreams as vivid but not scary, and didn't mention the nausea, which would go away on its own. They gave her generic advice and one mild dormo patch, then asked if she knew how to fix autodocs. The facility had six of them, to compensate for the distance to a full medical center, and one or another of them was always acting up. She had to profess ignorance and told the medics to contact the tech repair manager.

The CPS representative apologized for the need for a re-test, but she'd discovered the equipment had been miscalibrated in the previous test. At least she didn't ask for a free repair job.

Ferra didn't even bother to complain about this being the fourth time she'd been called in, each for a different excuse. It happened with all the indenturees, so she didn't feel singled out. She dutifully submitted to the measurements and tests, which again failed to discover any minder talent.

Non-minder indenturees assumed the rep was either padding her expense report or got a bonus for the number of tests. The fifteen or so minder indenturees got scut jobs and lived in segregated, higher-security cells. Plus, they had to take mandatory disruptor drugs to dull their talents. No one wanted to be identified as a minder.

In the tech repair office, she arrived just in time to be sent to the CRIO offices for an emergency call. Someone had breached their security to steal one of their deskcomps and smash the others. She salvaged what she could and replaced the rest with loaners. By the time she got back to Subcaptain Tauceti's office, she had to apologize for it being mid-afternoon, and six hours after she'd promised.

"Quite all right," he said. "How are you feeling?"

She smiled, once again charmed by his thoughtfulness. "According to the medics, my immune system is 'within acceptable parameters.'" She rolled her eyes. "They prescribed less stress, more exercise, and more sleep."

He smiled, and she felt like she'd won a gold star. Honestly, the man was dangerous.

She pointed to her bag. "I have parts for your wallcomp." Mindful of the multiple surveillance monitors, she frowned. "I have to put together a cart to bring the equipment I'll need to figure out all the things wrong with your deskcomp. The lab manager has to approve me taking it out. And parts printers are chained to the lab."

"Why don't I bring the deskcomp to your lab?"

"Are you sure? Argint d'Apa rules say you military people can't let your government tech out of custody. You'd have to stay." She could even quote the policy to him because she'd written it at lunchtime and inserted it into the lab's manual that no one had accessed in the last three years. *Come on, Tauceti, take the bait.*

He tapped his wrist gauntlet and looked at a display. "How about right after you finish with the wallcomp?"

"Sorry, I'm jammed until eighteen hundred." She tilted her head. "How about after the evening meal? I'm on call, but only for emergencies. Fewer interruptions." She gave him a lopsided smile. "Unless the chief scientist ditches his prized sample collection bot into a sinkhole again."

He frowned at the deskcomp and rubbed behind his ear, then glanced at the clock display.

She waved apologetically. "Never mind. You shouldn't have to give up your free evening just to get your tech working."

She put her bag down and popped the faceplate off the wallcomp. Maybe she could come up with some other way to lure Tauceti away from his fishbowl of an office.

She wanted to rip out the whole wallcomp and start over, but that was just frustration talking. It hadn't asked to be crippled by at least four different surveillance devices that tracked the sound, movement, power usage, and, previously, captured a video feed. "Poor little comp, you were just trying to do your job, weren't you?"

She used her company tablet to bring up a standard systems map for the wallcomp. She made the display big and visible to whoever was watching. Just a low-skilled tech, doing her job, cleaning out the non-regulation clutter.

She slowly and carefully removed each of the sensors, and dropped them into a shielded parts recycling bag. The sound monitor was the worst. Whoever installed it and its high-charge battery had been lucky not to flatline all the connected wallcomps in that wing or start a fire.

Maybe she could ask Tauceti to come to the indenturee gym to teach her how to use the ancient analog exercise equipment. *Right, because that didn't sound like a sleazy invitation at all.*

She'd been avoiding looking at Tauceti, because he deserved not to be interrupted, and she'd be distracted by the sinfully handsome scenery, but now she turned to him. "Try vocal commands for the wallcomp."

He paused the scrolling display of whatever he was reading. "Ceiling lights to fifty percent."

The lights dimmed.

"Restore ceiling lights."

The lights obligingly brightened to the previous setting.

A smile his face. "I'll try the other controls later."

She pointed her chin toward his desk. "I still need to test the touch controls." By which she meant, clear the crap out of those systems, too. "Is now a good time to displace you for about thirty minutes, or do you want to set an appointment?"

He glanced at the clock display. "Do I have to stay?"

"Uhm, the manual didn't say." She wanted him there because he made her feel safe, but she needed to get used to him being gone. "It's up to you."

Belatedly, she realized she couldn't remember if she'd been talking to herself, as usual. She'd probably annoyed him.

He stood and pointed to his deskcomp. "The search for the pertinent policies would take longer than it's going to take you to fix it. I'll stay." He moved his deskcomp to the high, narrow counter that ran the length of the office's far wall. "Use my chair if you'd like."

Twenty minutes later, she packed up her gear, including the three extra "bad parts" to be recycled. "Once I get the cart sorted, I'll ping you for an appointment to work on your deskcomp."

He cleared his throat. "I could bring it this evening."

She couldn't help but grin. "That's great. Nineteen hundred?" That should give her plenty of time to eat and clear the decks.

"Yes." He looked so serious that she wanted to ask what was wrong. *Get a grip, Barray.* Even if he told her, what could she do about it? She'd always been a soft touch for people in need, a trait her brother had exploited repeatedly until she finally wised up the hard way.

She settled for nodding and striding out of his office. In her experience, messengers didn't fare well when delivering bad news, and she imagined he wasn't going to like what she had to tell him at all. She imagined he wouldn't like this messenger much, after tonight.

5

Kedron's quest to recover his usual decisiveness failed. He hadn't found it in the military gym, the cafeteria, or his office.

He'd accepted Barray's invitation in a moment of weakness. Canceling was the right thing to do, but he couldn't make himself do it. The idea of spending more time alone with her felt too damn good, even if it was just watching her fix his benighted swamp slug of a deskcomp.

On the other hand, he could return her rescue crate and tell her to be more careful.

On the third hand, now that he was leaving, it didn't really matter if the deskcomp got fixed or not. His successor would probably get a new one anyway.

On the fourth hand—

Enough, he commanded himself. He scooped up the crate with the deskcomp and its accessories, ordered his office lights to twenty-five percent, and marched himself to the tech repair depot.

Ferra met him at the secure entryway and led him through an oddly-shaped suite with a maze of counters and shelves full of crates overflowing with parts-printer substrates. Their destination was a long, skinny room with windows all along one wall and a dizzying array of equipment crowded on every available surface. Some looked at least twenty years old. She had him put the yellow crate on a small gravcart.

"We're also the chair graveyard, so test anything before you sit down." She pointed to a bench next to the windows. "That's safe."

She emptied the crate and set it on the floor. Her efficient fingers quickly stripped the deskcomp down to essentials and inserted four longwires. She'd called herself non-adept, but her sure movements didn't sync with that description.

She pointed her chin toward the door. "Shut that, would you? Stray signals mess with the diagnostics."

He leaned over to press the control, and the door irised closed.

She shoved her hands in her vest pockets. "We have about ten minutes. This lab is tech-suppressed to the rafters." She blew out a noisy breath. "You're not going to like what I have to say, and I'm sorry, but I think you're as vector-straight as your record says, and you need to know. Your office has more overlapping, multi-factor, duplicate surveillance tech than a corporate spy showroom, and it's all aimed at you."

He blinked. He started to tell her she was wrong, but his brain engaged at the last second and stopped him.

First, she obviously knew a lot more about tech than

she let on, as evidenced by her trick with the perimeter fence. Second, she had nothing to gain from telling him, and had gone to the trouble of bringing him to a safe place to talk. Damn cleverly, too.

Lastly, he wouldn't put it past the military theft investigators to have installed the surveillance. More than one had doubted his innocence and ethics.

He tilted his head to look up at her. "How do you know what my record says?"

She raised an eyebrow and waved toward the whole wall full of percomps, deskcomps, and pieces of more comps, then put her hand back in her pocket.

Okay, it had been a stupid question. "Can you remove the surveillance?"

She leaned her hip on the counter. "Are you sure you want me to? It'll alert the watchers that you're aware of them." She glanced at the deskcomp on the cart. "Some of the tech looks old, some new. Maybe you have multiple watchers, which would explain the redundancies."

He tapped his fingers on his thigh. "The CRIO contract forbids Argint d'Apa's security from monitoring the government staff, but all that means is, 'don't get caught doing it.'"

She shook her head. "It's not standard company equipment. They monitor your office door, but that's likely emergency safety protocol."

"I wonder if I'm really the target. How far does it go? The CRIO or the CPS offices? My quarters? The whole government wing?"

She shrugged. "I didn't see anything in the CRIO

deskcomps that got thrashed this morning, but I wasn't looking. Break something else, and I will." She snorted. "Better yet, break that stupid CPS testing equipment so what's-her-name doesn't keep re-testing the non-minder indenturees every month."

"She does?" He shook his head. "Never mind." He considered the array of comps and tools on the long counter. "If I request a general tech assessment of the government wing in anticipation of an infrastructure upgrade, can you check for surveillance?"

"Sure, but my boss will probably assign one of the staff techs. I'm not allowed to do important stuff alone."

He thought a moment. "Do they work after hours? On call, like you?"

She laughed derisively. "You're kidding, right? Regular tech staff won't do shift work in the middle of a swamp. They all commute from Magloviti City. Even brilliant pay doesn't make up for the location. That's why Argint d'Apa applied for a CRIO partnership." She pointed to the wide, fluorescent green stripe on her uniform that clearly identified her as an indenturee. "They get cheap labor who can't leave. The CGC buys the rare metals the plant filters out of the runoff so they can build more interstellar ships. And if the scientists patent something from the swamp, the company makes a killing." Her expression turned sheepish, and her hands fluttered. "Sorry, I'll get off the bandwidth now."

"You don't approve of the CRIO system?" He'd never given it much thought until he'd been assigned as liaison.

She shrugged. "It's better than being sent as slave

labor on the stellar flux-particle collector stations, like the old Central League used to do, but CRIO is too much like pre-flight debtor's prison. 'Debt to society' should be more than numbers on a balance sheet." One of her eyebrows raised. "You don't see rich folk working for restitution fair wage or hunting for cleaning bots for the promise of a bounty."

"True enough." He happened to agree with her, but he needed to get back to the subject at hand. "I'll require the tech assessment to be done after hours."

"Better say 'preliminary' or something that sounds inconsequential. I'm not certified."

Steady beeping sounded. She turned and expanded a holo display on one of the counter deskcomps. "Show us what's ailin' ya', *leannan*." He didn't recognize the word, but her accent had a tinge of rural British Isles. Given her space-station origins, she probably picked up an eclectic vocabulary from all the major languages.

As she rotated the holo, he counted nine blinking red indicators. She brought up another holo and synced it with the first, so it rotated in tandem.

"Two of those"—she pointed to the blinking holo— "are simple soft-logic faults, but the rest are unauthorized add-ons, including a full data intercept. Which reminds me, your trouble reports never got seen or logged because they were marked as already completed. I think a previous staffer set up the routine to avoid the workload. If it makes you feel any better, yours weren't the only reports that got lost." She made a rude noise. "My boss is seriously torqued. You should see our queue now. Twenty months of backlog."

"Is my deskcomp worth cleaning up, or should I requisition a new one?"

"It's up to you." Her mouth twisted sideways. "The watcher obviously has free access to your office, so they may re-infect the deskcomp as soon as it comes back." She crossed her arms. "Yours has a military shell, but the internals are straight commercial. Our inventory says it came in with a previous liaison six years ago."

Guilt pinched him for not doing a security audit when he'd first been posted to Argint d'Apa. To be honest, he'd been going through the motions and feeling sorry for himself for two years, wondering what he could have done differently to save his career.

"Fix it for now. I'll tell the new liaison to order a replacement." An idea struck. He pointed to the military gauntlet on his arm. "Can you add tech that will alert my percomp if someone breaches the shell?"

"Maybe." Her eyes darted away. "Before this gig, I was just a hobbyist doing favors for friends."

He suspected that statement left out volumes of interesting truth, but he had no desire to interrogate or judge her. "It's okay. I'll just be happy to have tech that actually works."

"I sync that." She pointed out the window toward a battered workstation with a huge display. "If you want to kill time while I fix this, that has a direct uplink to the galactic net." Her irrepressible humor peeked through in her smile. "Leaves even the plant manager's pretty and pricey comp in the dust as far as speed."

He'd been planning to be suave and clever about returning the yellow crate to her, letting her figure out how he'd found it, but now it just seemed mean. She'd taken a huge chance, telling him about the surveillance, instead of turning a blind eye.

He cleared his throat. "Since we're in the place for delivering private news, I saw what you did at the fence last night." He waved toward the yellow crate. "I took the, er, contents farther away from the perimeter."

Her stricken look made him want to hug her. He shoved his hands under his thighs. "I only saw you because my window faces that direction, but it was a risky thing to do."

"I thought I'd be safe because of the lockdown." Tears welled in her eyes. "I'll find a different way, but I'm not leaving critters like that in the compound."

Even though he was just warning her, he felt like a heel. "Indenturee activities aren't my jurisdiction, and neither the plant nor the CRIO staff wants my input." He flicked his eyes toward the crate. "Rescue as many animals as you want."

"Thanks." She blinked her tears away. "Chaos, but I hate crying. Never does any good."

"If you don't mind telling me, how did you lift the fence?"

She pulled a multitool from her vest pocket. "I modified this to exploit a design flaw." She put the tool back. "Argint d'Apa and CRIO know about it, but they think no one else does, so they're in no hurry to spend the funds to replace it." Her mouth twisted. "Good thing Lambru and his sticky-fingered crew can't use it, or anything of value not fastened down would be on its way to every no-questions-asked market on the planet."

It was his day for surprises. "Marazzo Lambru? He's one of my current ex-military charges. I wouldn't have tagged him as a leader of anything."

Her expression hardened as she picked up a probe from the counter and bent over the guts of his deskcomp. "He's good at that. Likes to keep his hands clean."

While he waited on the bench, secretly entertained by the little conversations she had with parts of his deskcomp, he used his gauntlet percomp to look up Lambru's record. The high restitution debt resulting from his conviction as a blackmarket lab employee should have made him ineligible for a level-two facility like Argint d'Apa. However, the blackmarket pharma industry was awash with untraceable cashflow. It wouldn't be the first time that untraceable cashflow funds had changed hands to give an indenturee an easy-glide ride.

Kedron added Lambru to his private list of people who might want to know what he and the government staff were doing. He had the feeling it was going to be a depressingly long list.

———

6

Ferra wiped the mist off her face and handed certified technician Yolalo the R-685 module he'd asked for.

He placed it the socket, then used his tablet to tell the filter controller to connect to it. Before coming to Argint d'Apa, Ferra hadn't known water filters could be the size of a four-story building. A lucky quirk of geography meant the swamp collected runoff from the nearby mountains, where an ancient meteor strike had left exotic debris. By extracting the valuable rare metals, the plant made the swamp healthier, meaning downstream cities got more potable water.

Yolalo turned to Inzaya, the senior certified technician who watched the filter's readout. They both wore company-issue red rain slickers. Ferra only had her indenturee uniform. It felt like she was standing in a fog bank. If the water had been cascading down as usual, she'd have been drenched from the spray inside two minutes.

"I heard it was an interstellar escape pod." His accent hinted at Afro-French, and he affected an all-over gold skin tone, making him look like an illegally sentient android from a science-fiction serial. He collected sex partners the way some people collected novelty liquor bottles.

Inzaya, with her enviable dexterity and beautiful mahogany skin, shook her head. "Sensor is still flatlined. Try tracing the upline. I heard it was just a downed high-low flitter."

The whole compound buzzed with the news. The hunters and hellhounds hadn't yet found Healey, the escapee, but they had discovered wreckage and a body, the latter of which they'd managed to save from the icy spring runoff that flooded the swamp.

Yolalo opened a bigger panel, exposing more of the filter's tech systems. "Two longwires, gate class."

Ferra opened the tool cart's top drawer, found the correct compartment, and put the two longwires in Yolalo's waiting hand.

"Well, I saw what was left of the body after the swamp rats had been chewing on it for a week or two." He gave an exaggerated shudder. "You don't wear a space exosuit to fly a flitter."

Ferra dropped her head to hide her frustration. She was only supposed to have delivered the cart, not stand around and hand out parts like she was a pastry vendor.

Inzaya must have seen her. "Someplace else to be, *indenturee*?"

Ferra ordinarily would have kept her head down, but her work queue had doubled that morning.

Despite the dormo patch the night before, dreams of flying and being lost continued to plague her. During one of her waking periods, it occurred to her that she might be able to get a head start on Tauceti's project by combing through the newly unearthed trouble reports to look for tech failure patterns similar to those in his office. She couldn't work on the big plant equipment alone, but most of the trouble was in the staff and indenturee wings. The repair manager agreed to give her a restitution bonus for each backlog ticket she cleared.

"Yes, sir." Ferra gave her the military honorific. Inzaya had been in CGC Water Division decades ago and still used her former title from time to time. "The staff cafeteria payment kiosk, the security chief's receiving office, the staff immersion theatre, the military flitter stacker, the guard desk at the front gate, the—"

"All right, you've made your point," said Inzaya sourly. "Dismissed."

Ferra turned and walked quickly but carefully along the damp suspended walkway that led to the open-air lift to take her back to the ground floor. Good thing she'd never been afraid of heights, big turbines, or waterfalls of massive amounts of swamp water.

The pervasive humidity throughout the complex doomed her to perpetually frizzy hair for the duration of her indenture. The nearest body parlor or body shop was a hundred kilometers south, in Magloviti City. Indenturees were stuck with whatever mods they'd come in with, so she was glad her look was now all natural. None of her friends would recognize her. More importantly, none of her enemies would, either.

OF THE FIRST seven trouble spots on her list, one was a failed node, one was the result of a small bot trying to clean an electrical power bar, and five had the same surveillance tech infestation.

Someone had spent lavishly, but not wisely, and hired an incompetent person to install it. She made an executive decision to leave the tech in place unless it completely broke the system in which it was installed. No sense being the common denominator in the surveillance disruptions.

After Tauceti had gone away with his deskcomp, leaving the yellow crate with her, she'd spent the rest of her evening diving through Argint d'Apa data, which had surprisingly lax security. Maybe their physical isolation made them feel immune. No local company records mentioned the surveillance, or Tauceti by name.

The less accessible, but not totally crypto government records netted the same result, except the CRIO office copied Tauceti on every daily report, memo, and meeting recording they produced, regardless of how trivial. He dutifully copied them on every mind-numbing report and memo he produced. No wonder he looked forward to leaving.

As she restocked her bag and logged the completion of her last task for the shift, she decided to wait until morning to turn in the two small cleaning bots she'd found that day. She also contemplated skipping the evening meal and going straight to bed. Memories of her nightly dreams had invaded her thoughts all day, insinuating themselves into her idle moments.

Two distinct voices were scared and lonely, and desperately needed her help. She knew she had a weakness for being wanted and needed—her twisty brother had often taken advantage of that—but this felt different. And now that she finally had quiet time in the lab suitable for contemplation, it had a direction. South. And a persistent image to go with it, of posts, trees, and stacks of boxes.

Her job kept her busy all day, so she hadn't spent much time outside, but the trees in the image reminded her of the tall, droopy ones in the staff recreation yard, next to the tall fence that separated staff and indenturees. She'd heard complaints about them blocking the spring sunlight for the indenturee container gardens.

Despite her growing compulsion to go check, she couldn't just wander out to confirm her hallucination. She didn't know the area, so she'd be vulnerable if Lambru's remoras cornered her.

Too bad the gardens didn't have tech for her to fix, because they wouldn't bother her while she was on official business. She'd given them the impression that while on duty, a constant monitor listened to every word she said and tracked every location she visited. Both were true, but her work tablet did the listening, and the pass-tracker cuff got her past checkpoints and only actively reported her location when queried. As far as she knew, the repair lab manager hadn't looked at the logs in two months.

She put her tech bag on the shelf, then dimmed the

lights to half. One of the two bots she'd found had been charred, and its warning light blinked. "Yes, poor thing. I don't know how you got up on that counter, but maintenance will fix you up in the morning." And she'd get the bounty for returning them both.

Inspiration struck. She'd be on official business if she tracked an errant bot that just happened to go to the southeastern corner of the indenturee yard, near the trees.

She raised the lights to full and pulled one of the heavy, disused mobile repair bots out of the cabinet. They didn't do well in water, so the techs couldn't use them in the filtration plant, and they were too big for the smaller jobs typically assigned to her.

She named it Oran Mòr, because of its stylish orange stripes, and directed it to stick to the indenturee side, avoid people, and go to the southeast corner of the perimeter fence. Remembering the trick the maintenance tech had used, she added an asset tag under the maintenance door so she could use an inventory scanner to track it, in the event it got lost or waylaid. Some enterprising indenturee might mistake it for a cleaning bot and kidnap it for the bounty.

From the cabinets, she pulled out the large company-logo backpack and snugged the bot into it. She about fell over when she put the backpack on and tried to stand up. Wilderness hikers carried heavier packs, which meant they were even more warped than she'd thought.

The bot's little climbing feet dug into her back as she trudged down the corridor to the indenturee dining hall.

She had to show the backpack's contents to the guard to prove it wasn't contraband.

She paid for her mealpack, then took it out to the long, curving patio that overlooked the weedy indenturee courtyard. The landscaping looked half-finished to her, but what did she know? In space stations, plants grew in densely planned and orderly hydroponic gardens, and massive walls of moss supplemented the oxygen exchangers. Wherever she was going after her penance, it would be on a planet. She wasn't ever going back to living in space.

Luckily, none of Lambru's crew had followed her outside. Twilight brought chilly spring breezes. She put her mealpack on the farthest table, then set her backpack behind her on the ground, with the opening facing the grass. She put her tablet on the table, so she'd look busy, and dawdled over her meal of mixed meat and vegetable bits in a spicy sauce, covered in a layered pastry. She'd had worse growing up, but she'd since grown to love real food at real restaurants with happy people around her.

Through the windows, she kept an eye on the dining hall. The short-handed serving staff worked hard during meal service, because Argint d'Apa policy banned indenturees from kitchen-related jobs. She gathered it stemmed from an incident years before, when an indenturee got caught trading premium fresh food for sex. Indenturees were free to have as much consensual sex with each other as they wanted, but not with the staff. And apparently, the woman's preferred location for hot connects had been every available horizontal surface and wall in the pantry and prep area.

Ferra didn't miss sex as much as companionship and quality time friends who cared about her, and she wasn't likely get those in prison. All right, not prison, according to the CRIO system representatives, who assertively rejected any use of the word, but it sure felt like it to the indenturees. No other workplace she knew used plasma-powered fences, guards, and hellhounds to make the workers stay.

Her vest wasn't good protection from the chilly evening breeze. She used her tablet to check Oran Mòr's progress and found the bot was a good thirty meters from her.

Brushing off crumbs as she stood, she shouldered the now empty backpack, resisting the urge to turn and look behind her. She took her trash to the recycler, then slipped out the side door into the hallway for indenturee quarters. She walked past mostly closed doors to her own at the far north end, where she stopped long enough to put her warmest shirt on under her indenturee uniform tunic and utility vest. Back in the repair lab, she killed time by working on a solution for Tauceti to monitor his deskcomp.

The flaws in her plan became apparent after it took the bot a full hour to signal that it had reached the southeast corner. One, night had fallen, so she was going to need handlights and a shoulder torch to find her way, much less see if the frelling trees matched the persistent image in her head. Two, it was raining.

Now she couldn't leave Oran Mòr outside overnight, because of its vulnerability to water. She knew she shouldn't have named the little bot, because now she felt responsible for it. From the open office closet, she took out a red rain slicker and slipped into it, then pulled on the big backpack.

She tapped into her ever-simmering resentment at how Lambru got away with all manner of shit in the plant as she tromped down the main hall. The guards were more suspicious of happy indenturees.

The guard at the indenturee wing's south door made her walk through the metals detector and asked where she was going.

"Repair bot wandered off. Rain will ruin it." She brandished the inventory scanner. "This says it's outside by the container gardens, and I'm on call tonight."

"Better you than me." The guard waved her on through, then pointed to the hours-of-operation notice on the door. "If it's longer than fifteen minutes, you'll have to go around to the north entrance."

"Okay." She nodded her thanks as she pulled on her hood and switched on the high-lumen torch.

Every bench and shrub looked scarier in the dark. In the rain, the two moons did little to light the way. She walked carefully, wishing she had high-tech boots like Tauceti's. Her shoes had gripper soles for safety in the water-logged filtration plant environment, but the mesh uppers let in every drop of rain. Military people got all the best toys.

The standing white-legged boxes for the container gardens looked bigger than she remembered them from her first-day tour. Probably because she'd been surreptitiously eyeing the outrageously handsome Subcaptain instead of paying attention. She skirted around to the left, under the hanging tree branches. Slower, fatter raindrops drummed on her hood.

The closer she got to the corner of the fence, the more she became convinced she had visitors in her mind. Not telepaths, because they used words, and not empaths, because they were all about feelings. The two thought patterns were lost, and cold, and hurt. They'd called and called, and finally found someone to hear them.

Great, now she was dreaming while awake in the middle of a rainstorm.

She aimed the torch for the dark hulk that had to be the repair bot. Sure enough, there were Oran Mòr's orange stripes.

It turned its head, opened its eyes, and meowed softly.

You came.

Ferra nearly stumbled to her knees. The torch dropped to the ground and winked out.

A creature rose to its feet and shook water everywhere.

Help us.

A picture blossomed in her mind of another creature, waiting in the dark beyond the fence, unable to fly over it because of a broken wing.

She lit one of the small hand lights on her wrist. The creature in front of her stood knee-high at the shoulders and had the hint of an orange-striped bat-type wing folded flat along its side.

"You're real." It was all she could think to say.

The creature switched its long tail in annoyance.

Yes. Help us. Help him.

Once again, the image of the injured creature flashed in her mind.

Her wildest fantasies had never included sentient animals. It was too cold and damp to be a dream. And too cold and dangerous for an injured creature to be stuck outside.

She eyed the midnight-black creature. "If I raise the perimeter fence, can he crawl under?" She visualized the memory of lifting the fence to push the yellow crate outside.

Yes.

Edging closer to the inner fence, she considered her options. Somehow, she needed to get her multitool to the bottom of the fence line. Any human on the walkway would make the overhead lights come on. However, the motion sensors were trained to ignore animals, or the lights would be blinking on and off all night.

I can do it.

She looked down to see the creature sitting at her feet, looking up. The gold eyes mesmerized her for a moment. She got the impression the creature was female and anxious, and wanted comfort. Just like Ferra.

She gave herself a mental shake. Solve the problem. Deal with the mysteries later.

She fumbled under the rain slicker to find the vest pocket. She wrestled out the tool, selected the correct setting, and turned it on, then offered it to the creature.

We are not creatures. We are cats. Unmistakable pride accompanied the declaration.

"Of course you are," she whispered. "Everyone knows cats are telepaths and have wings."

The cat took the multitool in her mouth. *We are superior cats.*

The lithe cat oozed under the lower fence rail and streaked across the walkway, then dropped the multitool on the ground and batted it into place. The electrical fence lines warped upward in a semicircle.

Ferra took a deep breath for focus, then *pushed* through the multitool. She hadn't lied to Tauceti about how she lifted the fence, she'd just omitted the part about using telekinesis. She didn't trust anyone with *that* secret.

The cat crouched. The subtle light from the walkway's road glass reflected off her fur, making her hard to see, even though Ferra was only three meters away. In her mind, she heard the cat tell her mate to hurry. That's what he was, too, not just a companion.

A moment later, another winged cat, larger than the female, crawled through the opening. When the cat was all the way through, even his long, flat tail, Ferra released the fence. She sent an image to the female cat, asking her to bring back the tool.

The male cat limped across the walkway and slid under the inner fence rail. The female clawed the multitool away from the perimeter fence, then picked it up and trotted to where Ferra stood with the male.

Ferra crouched down to take the multitool. The male butted his wet head into her hand. The physical contact made the mental connection stronger. His wing and leg hurt. The breeze chilled him and his mate. The water was wet.

She smiled a little that his biggest gripe was about being wet. She sympathized. It had taken her several years of planet-side living to get used to water-based showers.

The cats couldn't stay out in the rain. Neither could the repair bot. She pictured her plan to the cats.

7

F erra shut her cell door, dimmed her lights, then slid the fully expanded backpack off her shoulders and set it carefully on the floor. She held it open for the remarkably patient cats to crawl out.

The universe, or perhaps the pre-flight Egyptian god of cats, granted extraordinary luck that night. She'd missed the south door operation window, so she'd had to trudge through the rain with twenty kilos of superior cats in her pack and twenty-five kilos of rain-slick repair bot hugged to her chest. She must have looked enough like a drowned swamp rat that the guard pointed her straight to the solardry and volunteered a gravcart for the bot.

The foreign thoughts and feelings in her head distracted her, but they also comforted her. She wasn't warped, twisted, or fracturing from loneliness.

The cats crouched and slunk around the small room, smelling everything. "I've got to take the bot and the backpack to the lab and return the cart." She didn't know how much they understood, but she projected images as best she was able.

The small female looked at her. *We will hide.*

"Good." She opened the tiny closet and even tinier fresher. On impulse, she crouched down and held out her hands to the cats. The male ignored her hand and went straight for her knee. He rubbed his triangular-shaped face against her. She stroked his damp fur. The female cat licked her outstretched fingers.

For no reason she could name, tears threatened, and she wanted to gather the cats in her arms. She reluctantly stood and stepped back. She dimmed the lights further, then locked the door behind her.

In the lab, she put a drying mat on the shelf, then put Oran Mòr on top of it and left the cabinet open. "I'll check you tomorrow," she told it. If cats could be sentient, so could bots.

No emergency trouble reports meant she could close up the lab, so she returned the gravcart and walked back to her cell. Worry tried to hurry her feet, but she walked sedately, then closed and locked the door behind her, just like any other evening.

The bed looked inviting, but first, she had to look after the cats. Their presence was warm and comforting in her mind, even if she couldn't see them. She used the wallcomp to turn up the lights and darken her only window.

The female oozed out from under the bed, followed by the male.

Now that she saw them in better light, she didn't know what she was looking at. Wide, cat-like heads and ears, with narrower muzzles, and nose flaps. Mottled dark fur with a faint rosette pattern, and folded, bat-style wings with fine downy fur. No orange stripe on the female's wing, so that must have been a trick of the light. Their front paws had sharp-looking claws and opposable toes. Their tails were long and ovoid.

We are cats. That was the female.

We were made for war, thought the male.

Food? asked the female.

Ferra didn't know what to do with cats designed for war, since the Central Galactic Concordance government had kept the peace across the galaxy for the last two centuries, but she could do something about food.

Reaching up to the top shelf of her closet, she retrieved the mealpack she'd stashed there two days ago. She triggered the heater and put it on a narrow counter that served as the cell's desk and table to warm.

She gratefully sat on the bed and pulled off her clammy shoes and tossed them onto the drying mat by the door. "Do you have names?"

The female's tale twitched. *Yes.*

Ferra laughed. The cat was just like some AIs Ferra had known, unhelpfully literal and disdainful of imprecise questions. Ferra tried again, this time forming the words in her mind and projecting them to the female cat. *What is your name?*

My call sign is Novo Seventeen Alpha.

I am Bozlurian Four Delta, volunteered the male.

"I'll just call you Novo and Boz, if you don't mind." She stripped off her damp socks stepped into the fresher to hang them in front of the ventilation grate.

When she came back, the mealpack signaled it was done, so she opened the lid and set it on the floor. "Sorry. No plates. You'll have to share. I hope you like protein egg straws and vat-grown ham."

She felt Novo's insistence that Boz eat his fill.

As he bolted down bites, Ferra sensed his hunger pangs being eased, the same way she could feel the constant pain in his wing and shoulder. She made a mental note to use the net uplink to look up vet med treatment protocols for cats and bats. Boz said they'd been designed, so she decided to check out pet trade references, too.

Chaos, but she was tired. She needed to think where to hide the cats while Boz healed, but her brain wasn't cooperating. She'd have to deal with it in the morning.

She stripped off her clothes and hung them in the closet. Her nose told her she'd soon need to book an appointment at the communal clothes sanitizer, or people would smell her coming.

She pulled on her nightshirt, then arranged a nest of spare blankets in the closet for the cats. If someone noticed it, they'd just assume she was a slob. She filled the licked-clean mealpack package with water from the fresher, told the cats goodnight, turned the light to low, and crawled into bed.

The next thing she knew, two furry bodies snuggled on either side of her, making rumbling noises in their throats. The cats projected comfort and relief, and the feeling of coming home again. She stroked their silky soft fur and cried for how scared and lonely they'd been.

For how lonely she'd been. Not just lately, but ever

since she was thirteen and her parents abandoned her and her twin brother on the space station and never came back. Ever since realizing she'd have to cut all ties with her brother because he'd drag her down with him. Ever since learning he'd sold her to a vicious, violent crew to pay off a gambling debt.

She fell asleep in purry, furry warmth.

8

After the evening of unsettling revelations, as Kedron had come to think of the repair-lab meeting with Barray, he'd spent a sleepless night wrestling with his choices, past and present.

He'd finally concluded that he'd learned the wrong lesson from his disastrous last post. He'd spent the last two years doing only his duty and nothing more, hoping HQ would call him back to his career. He'd been afraid that if he upset the sky skimmer again, his next assignment would be a fifty-year exploration expedition to the Great Void between the galaxies.

What he should have learned was that if his life plans didn't work out the way he hoped, he needed new plans. Not every Tauceti had to be a field commodore by age fifty, like his father, or have a galaxy-famous strategy named after him, like his great-great grandmother, who'd only retired three years ago at age one hundred and sixty-two. He could be the Tauceti who used his skulljack to train military hardware AIs how to work with humans, or made a quiet civilian military base run smoothly, or who had a family to come home to every night.

Since he no longer worried about making waves, he'd spent the last three days investigating the mystery of the source of the surveillance. He used the cover story of creating a comprehensive procedure manual for his position, which had never had one.

He'd also re-enabled his skulljack and started wearing a high-powered communications wire again. When he'd first arrived, the constant barrage of trivial communication between the various AIs in the plant had just about driven him around the bend. Almost anywhere else in the civilized galaxy, nonessential equipment used specific, reserved bands, but Argint d'Apa hadn't bothered, not even for the government offices. The compound was small enough that he could hear every system in it.

He could have requisitioned a filtered comms wire, but at the time, it had felt more fitting to simply disable his skulljack. As a consequence, he was out of practice and was still learning to pick out individual systems from the constant sea of noise. AIs were a chatty lot. The annoyance would be worth it if it helped him identify the watchers.

He'd already begun making appointments with people he interacted with, starting with the CRIO coordinator. He'd easily convinced her to approve the after-hours tech infrastructure assessment request, once he'd told her he'd volunteer to escort the technician and contribute from the military liaison budget to help pay for upgrades. He'd also discovered that he had authority over the CPS office suite. The Citizen Protection Service only admitted to being part of the military when it suited them, but he far outranked the local CPS representative. He simply notified her of the assessment.

Fortunately, the tech repair supervisor had obligingly assigned Barray, who would be starting the assessment that evening after her dinner.

At the appointed time, he met her at the guard checkpoint and escorted her to the CRIO office suite, to which he'd been given full access. Mindful of possible surveillance tech, he sat in a guest chair and pretended to read on his percomp.

Even though he'd had plenty of human interaction recently, he had to admit he still liked Barray's company best. She wanted nothing from him, and she made him laugh. With the theft ring situation, he'd had no one on his side except his assigned military advocate. At least this time, he had someone to trust, though he worried he might be putting her in danger.

Barray worked quickly around the office, using a scanner and her tablet. She looked more rested than she had a few days ago. He wanted to ask, but interaction might alert potential watchers to their friendly relationship.

No, not relationship. There would be no relationship-having with indenturees. Temporary alliance, maybe.

He distracted himself by asking the perimeter fence if it had detected anything unusual the night Barray had rescued the muskrats. The fence had a lot to say about all the animals and people it cataloged as proximate threats, but nothing about faults or disruptions. Unsurprisingly, the front gate's AI refused to communicate without an access code—couldn't have clever indenturees convincing the gate to let them out.

The interior perimeter path and lights shared an AI that reported a litany of complaints about mold and mud interfering with its sensors and ignored all nonhuman signatures.

All in all, it wasn't how he would have configured the security systems, but as Argint d'Apa's security chief had reminded—

"Subcaptain?"

He looked up to find Barray in front of him. The look on her face said she'd been waiting for him to respond. The downside to listening to machines is that he forgot to listen to people. "Yes?"

"Permission to use that chair to stand on?" She pointed to the chair next to him.

"Of course."

As she leaned over to pull the chair out, she dropped a small piece of paper in his lap. A flick of her eyes told him she'd done it on purpose.

It appeared to be a random list of locations throughout the complex. He used his percomp to take a quick flat image, then held up the list. "I think you dropped this."

She smiled ruefully. "Yep." She crossed from the large wallcomp to take it from him. "Sorry." She stuffed it in her vest pocket, then went back to climb on the chair and open the wallcomp's service door.

"No problem." He hoped that sounded casual

enough. He'd become hyper-aware of his actions, knowing he might be watched. With luck, his inherent stiffness would cover any gaffes.

On Barray's list, more than half had extra marks next to them. All had lines through them, except the bottom few, all in the CRIO office. The item at the top, his office, had the most extra marks. She'd said his office had a lot of surveillance tech. If she'd found more tech in the locations on the list, that meant that the majority of the company and government staff areas where tech could be found also had covert eyes and ears.

That gave a whole new dimension to his investigation. He'd been thinking small, like the company vice president negotiating the government contract renewal, or Lambru, who needed to know if the government had discovered his activities. Installing tech throughout the facility and having the time—or a sophisticated AI—to sift through the results, took considerably more resources. No fact had yet jumped out and tripped his finder sense as significant. He needed more data.

Barray pulled an instrument from her bag. "All right with you if I set up a tech suppressor for a few minutes?" She pointed toward his gauntlet. "You'll lose comms."

"Okay."

She touched the controls.

Silence reigned, except phantom echoes from his military-grade comms wire and the three office fans.

"Two minutes." She circled a finger. "Extras all around. Not like your office, but bad enough. This wallcomp is a mess." She smiled crookedly. "Even the portable fans have cameras."

"Any commonalities? The locations on your list seem random."

"Could be selection bias—I looked for trouble tickets like yours because I get a bonus for clearing them. The biggest commonality is the same model of camera. I've counted at least a dozen. The rest are incompatible and wrong-sized components, and they were spliced in wherever they'd fit. Whoever installed them knows even less about hardware tech than I do."

He frowned. "You are very knowledgeable."

"That's kind of you to say." She waved off his statement. "I know Argint d'Apa systems. I like reading, and taught myself the basics, because I didn't have anything better to do with my time and it kept me away from trouble." She pointed a thumb toward the wallcomp behind her. "Whoever did this is the kind of amateur you read about in the newstrends. 'Inventor Accidentally Flatlines Planetary Traffic Control System.'"

"Hmmm." Pesky facts didn't fit any of his theories.

"Since you didn't want me to remove the extras in your office, I've been fixing the trouble but leaving the tech in place, unless it caused the malfunction." She shook her head. "It still could be two different watchers, because some of the tech is done right."

She stepped off the chair to fish in her bag for a small multitool. "Before I kill the tech suppressor, this is for you." She slid it across the small conference table toward him. "Press the blue and red together twice and the light will blink if you're within a couple of meters of the surveillance cameras."

"Thank you." He pocketed it, touched by her thoughtfulness. On impulse, he added, "If you ever need help with a rescue, let me know." She was taking a lot of chances for him, so he could take one for her.

She blinked in surprise, then gave him a blinding smile. "I'll keep that in mind." She turned off the tech suppressor, closed up the wallcomp, and dragged the chair back into place. "I'm done in here. Where to next?"

It wasn't hard to pretend boredom as he followed her from room to room and finished up in the hallway. Barray hardly said a word, though her expressive face suggested she was still having running conversations with the tech she evaluated.

He hadn't allowed himself to watch Barray very much, because then he'd have wanted to talk to her. The woman in her written record didn't sync with the woman in person. Blame it on his finder talent, but he loved solving mysteries, and she definitely was an intriguing one. And, as he'd had to repeatedly remind himself, completely off-limits.

At the end of three hours, she slung her heavy tech bag over her shoulder. "My supervisor will send you the report."

"Any particular issues for upgrades?" That should be vague enough for the watchers.

He escorted her to the guard checkpoint.

She shrugged. "Humidity, mold, behind on maintenance. Like everything else in the plant." She snapped her fingers. "I forgot to mention, I found an old surplus fan, if the plant hasn't replaced yours."

"They haven't. I'll come get it tomorrow."

"I'll leave it in the lab with your name on it. If I'm not around, ask the tech no duty." She walked away, and he returned to the CRIO office to make sure he hadn't left a mess, then went to his quarters.

He wanted to try out the camera detector immediately, but he made himself wait until he could think of a way to disguise both it and his actions. The frustrating part was, even if it came up negative, that just meant no cameras. Barray had mentioned a half-dozen types of surveillance she'd found. Suddenly, sleeping in his military high-low flitter seemed very attractive.

Unless one of the watchers *was* the military, in which case, he may as well sleep in his comfortable bed.

9

F erra hoped Tauceti got the message she'd sent, and more importantly, figured out the hidden meaning. Otherwise, loitering after hours in the hallway near the government wing would be a magnet for guard suspicion, even though she was on official business. She didn't want to be memorable or appear in anyone's report.

Her quiet indenturee routine had become significantly more exciting since she'd rescued Novo and Boz.

She'd fallen in love with the cats when they'd cuddled and comforted her that first night. In her twilight dreams, the cats told her how they'd arrived on her proverbial doorstep. Their handler had been the dead man from the downed ship in the swamp. They'd all been undercover with an interstellar jack crew. After a betrayal, they'd barely made it out in an escape pod. Knowing he was dying, the handler released the cats and sent them to look for someone who could hear and help them. They'd found Ferra.

They'd nearly scared the life out of her the next morning when she could feel them in her head but couldn't find them. They'd appeared before her eyes in the pile of blankets, by way of demonstrating that their amazing fur put chameleons to shame. They could blend in with practically anything. It took conscious effort to drop the camouflage.

She'd since learned more of what cats of war could do. For one, they'd figured out how to get into the air-handling ducts in the facility, and into the garages intended for the maintenance bots. After examining the controls, she made tiny tokens for them to wear so any bot garage door would open for them. With luck, the plant's bot technician, Calderosh, would never notice.

For another, they'd told her where more small bots could be found so she could turn them in for the bounty. She was both amused and concerned when she started hearing rumors of the facility being overrun with giant blood-sucking bats or invaded by carnivorous miniature dinosaurs. Human science might have expanded their reach throughout the galaxy, but superstition was still alive and well.

She'd worried about feeding the cats, because she couldn't keep buying extra mealpacks without causing comment. Fortunately, they'd discovered the kitchen on their own and had been helping themselves to meal scraps ever since, but now, she worried they'd be caught. The sneaky, stealthy cats of war were insulted by her worry.

Ferra lucked out in not having to hide or explain net searches for veterinary medicine. Argint d'Apa had an entire hypercube of regular and pet-trade reference material in the huge indenturee library. It was one of many topics in the "career rehabilitation" section.

The most astonishing discovery she made was that she might have another minder talent besides telekinesis. According to the reference, a lot of vet meds in the pet-trade business were animal-affinity minders. Most were genera- or species-specific, such as horses or dogs. The best of them could mentally connect with and heal anything in a given clade, such as mammals. A very useful talent, considering the ethically challenged pet trade bred pretty much any fantasy animal they could sell— miniature dragons, hellhounds, or flying cats. Novo and Boz were likely experimental, or special order. Their creation was probably illegal, but she couldn't fault the military's actions, since it brought her the love of two superior cats.

The best news was that, while the Citizen Protection Service's Minder Corps aggressively recruited telepaths, telekinetics, healers, and sifters, they didn't have much use for animal-affinity minders. Not that she planned to march into the CPS office and ask to be tested. The Criminal Restitution and Indenture Obligation system reflected galactic society's suspicion of any minder, and enforced stricter security and separate, harsher justice for them.

Being an animal-affinity minder with a feline-family specialty explained why she could hear Novo and Boz so well, but had no connection to other animals, such as the genetically engineered hellhounds or natural young muskrats. It also explained why, when she touched Boz, she could sense the extent of his injury and his pain. Based on comparing anatomy images with what she could feel, he had sore and inflamed muscles, and maybe torn ligaments at the wing-shoulder joint. Easily repairable if she could sneak him into the veterinary medic autodoc in the dog kennel area and program it for a special cat, but she might as well wish for wings of her own.

The large clock display on the wall behind the guard station said Tauceti should be along soon. None of the clocks showed the whole planet, probably to avoid reminding indenturees and staff of anything outside Argint d'Apa. The paid staff turnover rate was almost on par with how often indenturees cycled in and out of the system.

The government wing door irised open to reveal Tauceti. She kept her expression bored, but she couldn't help but notice his body-skimming exercise clothes that fired her imagination. Nova hot didn't even begin to describe him. She didn't blame the guard for giving him a lingering, appreciative once-over.

Tauceti waved her through. "The force exerciser won't move at all."

The wing door irised closed behind them as they walked down the hall. She smiled a little at his explanation. Force exercisers weren't supposed to move. Credible lying wasn't in his skillset, apparently. A nice change from the indenturee company she currently kept, and her brother and his buddies.

Keeping her head down, she followed him into the military gym, where she set her bag on the force exerciser's seat.

The small gym had little surveillance tech, and at his request, she'd disabled all of it. She didn't blame him for wanting one safe place to himself. After checking the CRIO regulations, she'd done similar work in her cell, leaving only the emergency audio monitor in place. Argint d'Apa security couldn't very well ask the repair office to fix spy eyes that weren't supposed to be there in the first place.

He sat on a bench and looked up at her expectantly.

"I'll get straight to the point. I have a massive favor to ask."

Warmth drained from his expression as he stiffened. "What favor?"

She'd been so wrapped up in the needs of the cats that she'd forgotten her place, and his. Stupidity like that could destroy them both. "I'm sorry. Never mind."

She reached for the bag's strap. She'd find another—

"What favor?"

His bleak expression wasn't encouraging, but she'd already come this far. "I heard the military is sending you early to your new post, and that you're leaving in five days."

He looked startled, then shook his head. "I only got the orders this morning." Exasperation laced his tone.

"Once you notified the front office, everyone knew." It's what had given her the idea, in fact. "The favor is to take some animals away with you."

His eyes widened. "This is about a rescue? I suppose I could make a stop in the swamp on my flight out."

She shook her head. "No, I want you to take them with you to Merganukhan. You need to meet them to see why."

"I do?" Now he just looked perplexed.

She pulled her multitool out of her pocket and opened the wallcomp. After a moment, she used telekinesis to slide open the air handling grid in the ceiling.

Turning, she looked up in time to see Novo poke her head out. Her fur had taken on the mottled dull brown of the duct tubing but was already turning beige to match the ceiling by the time Tauceti followed her gaze.

Novo oozed out like an extrusion, then jumped to the ground with barely a thud. Boz followed, landing less gracefully. Both cats eyed Tauceti with keen interest.

For his part, Tauceti froze, then began shaking his head. "No, slow down. Wait. One at a time."

Ferra's jaw dropped. She could feel the cats talking to Tauceti, but not with the mind speech they used with her. It felt weird.

Novo sat in front of Tauceti and stared unblinkingly into his eyes.

Boz limped over to Ferra and rubbed his head on her knee. *He is a military controller. Our controllers sync with him.*

She crouched to rub Boz's rounded, mobile ears, which he liked. *Controllers?* She'd gotten better at talking with her mind instead of her mouth.

The tech in our heads. Ask Novo. Boz padded over to sit in front of Tauceti.

Novo drifted by Ferra briefly, then began investigating the equipment in the room, looking and sniffing. *We have military computers in our brains. You do not. He does. We can report to him, but he can't feel us like you do.*

Ferra looked at Tauceti and remembered his question about a skulljack, and how he rubbed behind his left ear when thinking. It made sense that not all military personnel with skulljacks would wear tattoos that lit up and pointed to them, like elite forces Jumpers did.

Tauceti looked up to meet her gaze. "You bonded with them." His neutral tone gave nothing away as far as his feelings.

She shrugged. "They needed my help."

"Their former handler, Galagade, the pilot who died, worked for the Minder Corps as a covert operative. The cats' comps say they are stealth weapons and think I'm their new handler. The comps think I'm the animal-affinity minder who bonded with them. The cats say otherwise."

She appreciated that he'd avoided accusing her of being a minder, but it didn't solve the problem.

"I can't be a handler. I'm an indenturee. I've got another two or three months to go, depending on how many extra shifts and bounties I get." She made an exasperated noise. "They're not safe here, despite their chameleon fur and skulking skills. The guards would love to throw them to the hellhounds."

Novo circled back to rub against Ferra's leg. *We can fight.*

Ferra shied away from the image. She'd seen what the hellhounds could do. "You're their only hope for getting out of here, especially since you can hear them. I was hoping you could board them someplace on Merganukhan until I can come for them. I can pay."

He shook his head. "Pets are strictly forbidden on Space Div military transports." Boz, the petting junkie, had already wedged his muzzle into Tauceti's hand. "Besides, Minder Corps probably wants them returned."

Ferra shuddered. "I'll turn them loose in the swamp before I'll send them back there. Once they'd connected with Galagade, the researchers experimented on all three of them, trying to break the bond, and it hurt. They'd probably still be in the labs, except Galagade had family in high places. The CPS transferred him and the cats to the sneaky spying and theft division." She waved toward the cat currently perched on top of the free-weight stacker. "At least, that's my interpretation of Novo's story."

He shrugged a shoulder apologetically. "Even if I was a subgeneral instead of a subcaptain, Space Div wouldn't let me bring them on board."

"What if you were a courier for a top-secret project?" She shoved her hands in her pockets and rocked on her heels. "I can make it so in the records. I can say they're lethal or communicable, so no one wants to get within five meters of them."

He raised an eyebrow but said nothing.

Time to do what was right for the cats. "That's how I sent myself here."

His eyes widened. "You came here on *purpose*?"

"I needed to vanish, fast. I know it sounds crazy, but the CRIO system seemed the safer alternative at the time." She blew out a noisy sigh. "I'm a... I *was* a top-level financial systems integrator, working for one of the big galactic information exchanges. I refused to bail my brother out of trouble for the umpteenth last time. He lured me to a meeting, supposedly to say goodbye. Turned out he'd sold me like I was exotic fresh fruit to the big, powerful crew he owed a lot of money to." Chaos, but that final betrayal still hurt. "The crew needed someone with my skills to move their money and hide their trail. I convinced them I'd signed on willingly, so they didn't watch me like they should have. I escaped, but they were hot on my afterburner, so I couldn't go anywhere near my former life. I used my data manipulation skills to steal pieces of records to make a new identity, insert me into the CRIO system, and vanish." She blinked to keep the tears from falling. "I can do the same for the cats."

Novo jumped down to the floor, using her wings to keep her from making a thud.

"Why didn't you go to the planetary police, or the CGC military detectives?"

She sighed. "I panicked. I didn't know anyone in law enforcement—maybe the crew had them on payroll, too." She shook her head. "I deserved to do time for trusting my brother one more time, even though I'd told him to not even send me a fucking birthday message ever again." Honesty made her tell him the idea that had occurred to her yesterday. "It's possible they found me and paid someone to install the surveillance tech. To them, I'm like that runaway cleaning bot the other day—misbehaving property to retrieve and keep better track of this time."

He frowned as he continued to pet a loudly purring Boz. "I thought you said the tech has been around for at least a year. You've been here less than four months."

"Some is old, some is new. Still could be two sources." She made a frustrated sound. "I can't take the cats with me until I know it's safe."

Novo leaned against Ferra's legs. *We will teach you to hide.*

Ferra sat on the force exerciser's frame and leaned over to stroke Nova's downy fur. *Thank you. We'll think of something.*

Tauceti's expression turned bleak again. "I'm not safe, either." He frowned and looked away, a troubled expression on his face. The hand petting Boz stilled. "At my last post, I blew the whistle on a theft ring. The military sent me here for my safety, but some of the investigators suspected I was part of it. They refused to believe that I had absolute zero personal relationship with the commodore, despite her insistence we were lovers." He swallowed and looked down. "I'm not built that way. I don't make friends easily, so I had no one to tell when she pressured me. If I had slept with her, I don't know that I would have told them, anyway. I didn't want to be known as the Tauceti who used hot-connect sex to get promoted."

"Chaos, that tanks." She wanted to comfort him, but that was impossible. The past couldn't be changed. She shoved her free hand in her vest pocket and made a fist, wanting to deck whoever had hurt him so badly. No wonder her clumsy request for a favor had rocked him so hard.

"What I'm saying is that I'm no safer for the cats than you are. The surveillance could be the military investigators watching me, hoping I'll make a mistake." He put his hands flat on his thighs. "If they caught you tampering with my records, they'd send you to military prison for decades."

His defeated look matched the way she felt.

"I apologize for involving you in this." She stood and brushed a few hairs off the front of her uniform.

She aimed thoughts at Novo and Boz. *Let's go. I snagged a nice meaty mealpack for you tonight.*

She watched as they jumped to the top of the exercise equipment, then launched unerringly into the tube that looked too small. They were truly amazing creatures.

Superior cats, thought Novo.

Yes, you are, Ferra sent, as she slid the wallcomp door shut and again used her teke to close the ceiling grate.

She turned to Tauceti and tried to memorize his too-handsome face, his still-troubled face. She'd deal with the pain of losing him later. "I probably won't see you again before you leave. Best of luck at your new base on Merganukhan." She smiled briefly. "I'll always remember the planet's real name of 'Suck Flux, RSI.'"

She scooped up her tech bag and stood by the door until he stood and opened it with a wave of his hand.

They walked silently down the corridor to the end of the hall, where the door irised open.

For the sake of their guard audience, she gave Tauceti a slightly peevish look. "Next time, try not to move the force exerciser. It's not built for it."

Tauceti nodded gravely but said nothing.

Ferra trudged off, feeling the weight of the world on her shoulders. Well, the weight of two light-boned cats, anyway.

10

"What I wouldn't give to be in your place." Soares, the CRIO coordinator, gave Kedron a wide, envious smile. "Getting off this stinking planet tomorrow and back to civilization again."

She'd invited herself to sit with Kedron at the midday meal. The Argint d'Apa security chief had invited him out to dinner that evening in Magloviti City. Odd how they only considered him worth talking to now that he was leaving.

His new policy of honesty with himself made him admit he could have engaged with them and the others when he'd first arrived, and perhaps made friends.

Kedron nodded and gave Soares a polite smile in return. "High Command could still change their minds again."

Soares laughed. "Good point. Don't jinx fortune by counting your cashflow chips before you have them in hand."

Kedron should have been as happy as Soares

apparently assumed he was, but he'd spent the previous four days wishing he could stay longer. He'd come up with one idea for Barray's cats and sent it to her via the command processors in the cats' heads, for one of them to relay to her. But other than removing one obvious threat, he had no ideas on how to protect the woman herself.

Not that it was any of his business to do so, but he felt responsible. He'd involved her in his investigation into the surveillance source. The fact that he'd failed to find it left her vulnerable to whoever was behind it. She'd trusted him, and he'd let her down.

Soares finished the last swallow of coffee. "Any idea who's replacing you?"

"No," he said. "I'm lucky that High Command remembered to send me the updated transfer orders with the earlier departure date."

Soares laughed again. "That's the government for you." Her bracelet-style percomp blinked. "Gotta run. I'll see you tomorrow to say goodbye."

She took her tray and left him alone once more. He might have felt it more keenly, but the kitchen and dining hall AIs murmured in his head, something about canine treats for an audit. AIs usually knew about surprise inspections before any of their human counterparts. He'd used it to his advantage more than once in his career to avoid a red flag or two from overzealous inspectors.

After dropping his tray in the recycler, he headed toward the building's shipping section to check on his little-used military high-low flitter. Tomorrow, he'd fly it to the planet's only military base and space port, on the next continent to the west, and leave it for his successor.

He used the comms wire in his skulljack to direct the shipping pad's flitter stacker to release the flitter into the separate military hangar, which was little more than a garage. The AI complied, but warned him it couldn't accept it again until after the upcoming maintenance cycle that would put it and the traffic controller out of commission.

His finder sense flashed an alarm. He detoured to a nearby fresher and sealed the door, then queried the rest of the AIs in the complex. Suspicion confirmed, he closed his eyes and filtered through the hundreds of signals until he found the two he was looking for.

Novo, Boz. Find someplace to hide from an all-facility lockdown and inspection. It starts at 0930 hours. They're calling it a training exercise in the records, but they're actually looking for illegal chems, and they'll be using both the dogs and hellhounds in a room-by-room search. Warn Barray.

He hoped the cats got the message, because he didn't know how to make their controller wake them. He'd deliberately avoided getting to know the cats after their introduction, convincing himself it wouldn't be fair to them.

Now, he saw his behavior for what it was—his old, bad habit of avoiding the possibility of pain by pulling inside his turtle shell. One he needed to break.

He enjoyed solitude from time to time, but not all the time. He liked meeting extraordinary cats, and getting to know smart, laughing women, or at least one in particular. He'd be lying to himself again if he denied he already felt an emotional connection with her.

Their current circumstances weren't their lot in life, they were only temporary. The likelihood they would meet again by chance was incalculably remote, but he could change that, if he had the courage.

Remotely, he checked that his comms wire connected properly to the flitter, ensured its general status was green-go, and left it in the hangar for tomorrow. He walked briskly back to his office, stopping at the guard station along the way to borrow a gravcart. He filled the cart with all the portable tech from his office, even the replacement fan, then presented himself at the tech repair office secure entryway and pinged until someone answered.

A gold-skinned technician whose company name tag read "Yolalo" let him into the office. He frowned suspiciously at the gravcart's contents. "What's all that?"

"Tech from my office. I'm flying out tomorrow. *My* procedure says military government tech has to be secured for my successor." Yolalo didn't need to know he'd learned from Barray's tactics and written the procedure himself just a few minutes ago. "*Your* policy says I have to bring it to you for chain of custody."

Yolalo grunted and turned toward the back. "Barray! Customer."

When no one answered, Yolalo muttered about no one ever being around to do their jobs. He unloaded the cart, recorded the asset tags, and locked them all in a sealed container.

Kedron used his wait time to query the repair depot's

AI about the locations of all its self-directed mobile repair components, which was how it categorized the human repair technicians. He couldn't do so from outside the office because of all the shielding and tech suppressors.

Unsurprisingly, the technicians were scattered all over the building. Barray turned out to be in the filtration plant, on the top walkway above one of the gigantic filters.

His plan to accidentally run into her just in time for the lockdown would have to wait until she came back. Unless...

He headed toward the plant. As he walked, he called up the liaison manual on his military percomp to add a new procedure.

11

F erra would have kicked herself for being so blazingly stupid as to get cornered by Lambru's remoras in the filtration plant, but she needed all her energy to avoid getting hurt or worse.

She'd been with Tech Inzaya on the bottom level, helping fix the lift controls. Inzaya sent Ferra to the top level, then got called away. Ferra had already tagged the presence of several of Lambru's crew working in other areas. The moment Inzaya left, they'd started to move toward Ferra's location. She'd be a fool to think it was just coincidence.

She'd need wings to get to the open side windows. The big powered lift couldn't move until the bottom-level control panel freed it. She could barricade herself in it, but "lift accident" made a pithy title for an injury report. So did "accidental fall," which was why she opened the cage for the emergency ladder. It was little more than rungs on a giant articulated chain, but it would get her down safely.

Except it was already in use by a well-muscled black-haired woman manually climbing up it. "Heyo, Indenturee Barray, what's the rush?" She sneered. "Too good for the likes of us who actually *work* for our restitution?"

Ferra held her hands up and backed up, putting the lift at her back. She didn't have long to wait.

Lambru himself arrived with the three other remoras. "Don't bother calling for help. The repair tech monitors can't hear you in here." He opened the front of his indenture uniform to reveal a tech suppressor in his floral undershirt pocket. As was apparently his habit, he got right to the point. "You moved yourself from nonentity to competition when you stole my stash of cleaning bots."

"Bots?" She didn't have to pretend confusion. "I thought you wanted me to steal tech."

Lambru's eyes narrowed. "I hate liars." He pointed a curling finger at her. "You've been seen with *my* bots every day this past week." He pointed to her pass-tracker cuff. "Very crafty, using that to get by the guards to sell *my* product to the staff."

Ferra shook her head. "I hunted cleaning bots for the bounty that technician Calderosh told me about. I don't know shit about your product. I haven't sold anything to anyone."

"Hmmm. Let's pretend I believe you for the moment." He tapped pursed lips with a metallic-pink fingernail. "Your previous lack of cooperation represents lost-opportunity costs that require personal restitution." He pointed to her tech bag. "I'll take that, for starters."

We are coming. Boz was in her head.

No, she thought furiously. *They'll hurt you.*

She dipped her shoulder and let the bag slip down. It landed half on the catwalk grate, at the edge of the open lift. "It's all yours. Might be hard to explain at the checkpoint."

Lambru gave her an oily smile. "You let us worry about that. Your pass-tracker, too."

Suddenly, blue and red lights began flashing, accompanied by an ear-splitting alarm. An automated voice blared from everywhere.

"Attention, all personnel. This is an all-facility security lockdown. Stay where you are until further notice. You may only move if your present location is unsafe. Motion detection commencing. Tracker location audit commencing. Filtration turbine shutdown commencing. Follow orders. Do not interfere with the guards or the dogs."

"Fuck," said the black-haired woman. She looked to Lambru. Two of the crew ignored the announcement and took off at a run down the catwalk.

The blaring announcement repeated, making Ferra's ears ring.

The irises over the roof skylights began to close. The walkway darkened.

Behind Ferra, the lift suddenly jerked to life. When its safety gate encountered her tech bag, it sounded a loud, buzzing alarm. She eyed the gap.

Lambru lunged forward to grab Ferra's arm and kick the bag into the lift. The gate closed. The lift sank out of sight.

He grabbed the back of her neck hard, hauled her to the edge of the walkway, and forced her to look down at the waterfall. "If you cross me, you'll be taking a swim, just like indenturee Healey." He grabbed the flesh at her waist and gave it a hard, twisting pinch. "She didn't even make it past the filtration pump before she died."

He forced her down. His fingernails gouged into her skin. The walkway grate dug into her knees.

She reached out for the cats to tell them to stay with Tauceti. He was a good man. He would keep them safe.

Lambru turned to his three remaining remoras. "You two, go block the other two lifts on this side. Durga, block the ladder. We're up here to rescue Indenturee Barray, who got stranded up here in the lockdown." The crew trotted off to carry out his orders.

He tightened his grip cruelly until Ferra cried out in pain. "Stay." He shook her neck twice, then released her.

The chest-deep vibration of the gigantic turbine changed pitch. The waterfall of swamp water slowed. The shadows deepened as the skylights closed.

If Lambru was going to toss her over, he'd have to do it quickly. Her heart raced, and she wanted to throw up. Just like when her brother abandoned her to the mercy of the jack crew. She didn't know how to talk her way out of this one.

You are not alone. Novo's thoughts flooded her with fierce anger and fiercer love.

Ferra's eyes ached with unshed tears. *Thank you for that.*

The walkway vibrated briefly. From her position

looking down, she saw the lift start to rise from the ground level.

Lambru noticed, too. He warned Durga, who was standing at the emergency ladder, then turned a threatening glare on Ferra and made a "lips zipped" gesture across his mouth.

By the time the lift arrived, Lambru had turned off his tech suppressor and was the picture of fluttering, ineffectual concern. He needn't have bothered, because the lift's lights showed it had nothing in it, not even her tech bag.

Lambru swore and stomped to the railing and leaned over to peer down at the lift column's base.

The vibration of the turbine faded. The waterfall's volume decreased.

Durga cried out. "What was that?"

"What?" demanded Lambru, turning to look.

"Something flew by and pulled my hair." She moved closer to the uprights of the cage, looking fearfully upward into the shadows. "This is where the vampire bats live. They think it's night."

"There's no such—" He screamed and stumbled backward, holding his face. Blood seeped through his fingers.

Duck, ordered Novo.

Ferra sat on her heels and bent over to cover her head.

She peeked to see Boz climbing over the railing, his fur color rippling to match the shadows and crosshatch gray of the screening.

Durga screamed again and scrambled onto the emergency ladder and began climbing down. An eerie keening arose, causing Durga to whimper and descend faster.

Lambru fumbled with something inside his tunic. The deep claw marks on his face dripped red. The naked snarl on his face foretold violence.

Boz leapt onto the man's back, digging in with sharp claws and yowling with anger. Lambru howled. Ferra used her teke to nudge Lambru's stumbling feet. He tripped and fell to his hands and knees, which threw Boz off his back.

Boz opened his wings and flew upward, but she could feel his pain. He couldn't last.

Hide, Ferra told him.

The plant's automatic inside lighting finally snapped on.

Lambru pulled a small stunner out of his tunic and spun around, ready to shoot, but found no target. He aimed the stunner at Ferra. "What are those things?"

Ferra shook her head violently, letting him see her terror.

He used his sleeve to wipe the blood off his face.

Behind him, as if from nowhere, Subcaptain Tauceti climbed quickly and silently over the railing and onto the walkway.

Ferra concentrated her teke on Lambru's hand and pushed with everything she had. The stunner arced up and landed on the walkway.

Before Lambru finished his vicious oath, Tauceti jabbed him with a stick. Lambru stiffened, then crumpled like a deflated balloon.

Tauceti stepped over him to crouch close to Ferra. "Can you move?"

She sat up, feeling bilious, but that was better than feeling dead. "Yes. How did you get up here?"

He stepped back while she stood. "I hung on underneath the lift." He collapsed the stick and slipped it into his thigh pocket.

She edged away from Lambru's body. "What did you hit him with?"

"Military shockstick." He quick-stepped down the walkway to scoop up the fallen stunner and drop it in his uniform chest pocket. "The lockdown is still in force." He crossed back to search Lambru's body and confiscate two more weapons and the tech suppressor.

Her spirits sank. "Do I have to stay here, then?" She shoved her hands in her vest pockets to hide the trembling. Between the adrenaline aftermath and the blowback nausea from overusing her lightweight telekinetic talent, she was a mess.

"No." He invited her into the lift with a wave of his hand, then followed her in and closed the gate. The lift descended.

He looked at his feet. "To be honest, I was hoping to get stuck with you."

She squinted at him. That made no sense, so she focused on the more immediate problem. "What about Lambru?"

"He's being transferred." Tauceti's smile had a hint of predator. "I'm responsible for all military indenturees. I arranged a slot at a higher-level CRIO facility. At his present restitution rate, he'll need another eighty years to pay his debt. The CRIO system isn't meant to be a lifelong career."

She touched her neck and winced, then looked at the blood on her fingers. Her stomach churned.

Tauceti's smile faded. "I've just decided Lambru will be leaving tomorrow, with me. He's not safe here."

"He's, uhm, hurt." She mimed a cat's claw down the side of her face. She couldn't think of anything in that part of the plant that could plausibly cause those injuries. Lambru would scream about being attacked by something, even if he hadn't seen it.

Tauceti nodded. "I'll make sure he gets treated in the big autodoc before we go. Twilight drugs sometimes give patients vivid dreams."

The lift arrived at the ground floor. When they stepped out, two guards with a leashed hellhound approached them. "Lockdown means everyone, *amigo*."

Tauceti pointed upward. "Call the medics and bring a gravcart. There is an injured person on the top walkway."

Ferra had never seen the command side of Tauceti. She wasn't surprised the guards looked at him with careful regard.

The guard not holding the hellhound leash touched her earwire and subvocalized. After a brief conversation, she nodded, then turned to Tauceti. "The Sec Chief respectfully asks you to confine yourself to the military area until we've concluded the search."

Tauceti nodded. "Very well. Barray will be with me."

"Indenturees aren't..." The guard trailed off.

Tauceti's forbidding expression would have stopped a squad of Jumpers in their tracks.

"Okay, then," said the guard. She nudged her partner. "May as well start up top."

On impulse, Ferra reached out with her newfound animal-affinity talent to see if she could sense the hellhound. She thought she felt its presence as an entity, but nothing of its thoughts or emotions. She needed practice.

They are drooling puppies, said Novo in her head. The image of a hellhound baying at the two moons accompanied the disdainful thought.

Ferra dropped her head to hide her smile. *Says the superior cat who chases her own tail.*

K edron showed Barray where he'd stashed her tech bag, then led the way through the main plant doors. Instead of going down the long hall to the government wing, he turned left, into the shipping area and out onto the flitter pad. He led her into the small hangar and sealed the door behind them. Technically, it was a military area.

The high-low flitter took up most of the room. He opened the flitter's side door, then gestured inside. "It's the only place to sit."

She walked up the shallow ramp and stepped inside, only to be nearly tripped by two spotted, winged cats twining about her legs. She laughed as she waded through cats to get to the bench on the far side. The moment she dropped her bag and sat, Boz draped himself across her lap like a rug. Novo put her front paws on Barray's knees and presented her chin to be rubbed. "You are both treasures."

Kedron was glad he'd remotely retracted the hangar's

roof and opened the flitter's skylight for the cats. He leaned against the entryway and watched the reunion. Barray's happiness made him smile, too.

Her earlier fear had cut him like a knife. Her injuries were partly his fault. He should have removed Lambru the first day he'd thought of the way to do it, not waited for the CRIO system to respond to the order.

"Thank you for what you did. You and the wee beasties." Nova dropped to all fours and licked her own leg.

"They felt your distress and alerted me. I'm glad we got to you in time."

"Me, too." She smiled up at him. "You even look heroic just standing there. You should be in military recruiting posters throughout the galaxy." She blushed and looked away. "Sorry, that was inappropriate."

His face burned with a blush of his own. "I was, actually. When I was a sixteen-year-old cadet. I hated it."

Her eyes widened in surprise. After a moment, she nodded once. "The other cadets teased you mercilessly, didn't they?"

Novo's attention focused on something outside the flitter. In a flash, she launched herself past Kedron's legs. He turned to look, but the cat had vanished. No wonder their processors identified them as stealth weapons.

"They did." He'd had no idea what he'd been letting himself in for. Most people assumed it had been his ticket to fame. She was the first person he'd told who'd understood.

She smiled sympathetically. "When we were fourteen, my twin brother and I topped the local newstrends for a few months as the prize-winning holo image in an exposé about the secret world of abandoned children on space stations." She made a rude sound. "Secret, my ass. We were wards of the government, living in group dorms. I changed my look as soon as I could afford a body parlor, so I wouldn't be that kid anymore." She pulled out a strand of dark wavy hair. "I haven't looked like this in fifteen years."

He stepped further inside the flitter and watched her stroking Boz's shoulder and wing. "What did you think of my idea on what to do about your treasures?"

"Idea?"

"I sent them a message three days ago to relay to you."

She looked down at Boz, who swiveled an ear and twitched his tail. She frowned, then looked up again. "They won't tell me."

Kedron suspected they didn't want to leave her. He knew the feeling. "I could ship them to me via a commercial transport and mark the container as live scientific samples."

"From what I've read, that's how the pet trade used to smuggle their wares, so now, eco-inspectors open every container. That's why..."

She trailed off and her eyes widened.

Novo trotted past him carrying a small, struggling cleaning bot in her mouth. She dropped it at Barray's feet. When it righted itself and started to move, Novo stopped it with her paw.

Barray laughed as she gently urged Boz off her lap,

then picked up the cleaning bot. "My restitution account thanks you."

Novo went back out the door. Boz stretched out on the end of the padded bench. His fur color rippled into a pattern that made him look like a carelessly wadded-up blanket. The cats truly were remarkable.

Kedron watched as Barray pulled out her multitool and opened the bot's service port. She touched something inside, and the bot stopped waving its rollers.

Second thoughts about his plan to talk to her about the future tied his tongue. He still had authority over her. Maybe she'd think he'd retaliate if he didn't like her answer. And once again, he was expecting her to take all the chances. "Is it too late to make me a courier?"

Ferra held up the little bot to the light and peered into its interior. "Hmmm?"

"What are you doing to my bot?"

Startled, Kedron turned to see Calderosh, the maintenance tech, standing in the entry of the flitter. He hadn't heard her approach. He hadn't even heard the door.

"Your bot?" Kedron asked.

Ferra put the bot back in her lap and closed its port.

Calderosh held out her hand. "I'll take it off your hands, if you'd like."

Ferra held the bot as she put her multitool in her pocket. "No, I'm good, thanks. I'll give it to my boss, so I get the bonus."

Calderosh produced a very lethal hand-beamer from her pocket. "I insist."

She edged in, covering both Ferra and Kedron. She couldn't miss at that distance. "Hand it over. Easy."

Ferra slowly leaned forward to put the bot in Calderosh's hand, then sat back down on the bench.

Calderosh curled her arm to hold the bot against her ribs. She waved the beamer toward Kedron. "So, what's this about treasure and a courier?"

He kept his face neutral and said nothing. He reached out to the cats. Once again, they couldn't go for help, so they'd have to *be* the help.

Calderosh hissed in annoyance. "I thought it was my lucky day when the famous Subcaptain Kedron Tau landed here and I found out about M'Tendere's missing treasure. All my data-broker contacts said you were her number-one boytoy. I thought you were just laying low, waiting until the meteor storm passed." She rolled her eyes. "But no. You are the most boring man on the planet. After two years of watching and waiting for you to leak significant information, I deserve a frickin' medal." She aimed the beamer at Barray's knees, the threat implicit as she glared at him. "So, tell me about the goddamn treasure."

Barray sighed loudly. "It's a pet-trade shipment. One of the scientists has a side gig, designing unlicensed hybrids for a pet-trade company." She pointed to the bot. "Just like your bots, indenturees are everywhere, and no one notices us. I overheard the arrangements for a live shipment for tomorrow." She frowned sourly and pointed a thumb in his direction. "Since Subcaptain Perfect is also leaving tomorrow, I was trying to convince him to intercept it and act as a courier, so I can pay off my restitution early."

Although he probably shouldn't have, Kedron admired her ability to weave a lot of little truths into one big lie.

Novo's controller requested orders on whether or not to kill Calderosh.

Disable only. They had enough trouble without explaining a dead body.

He suddenly noticed both women were looking at him. He frowned sternly and shook his head. "Pets are not allowed on military transports."

Calderosh's expression turned thoughtful. "What kind of pets? None of Lambru's spy eyes recorded any pets."

Barray shrugged. "Dunno. I know the shipment weighs twenty-two kilos. How did Lambru get surveillance tech in the government wing?"

Calderosh shrugged. "Hired people, probably. Lots of personnel turnover here, which is good business for me. My bots found the fresher where he hid the central data collection hub, so I modified the AI to delete anything with me and my bots. Which was a mistake, because it took me a while to figure out Lambru was stealing them to send them along the ducts with his crappy home-brew recreational chems. They're what killed that indenturee, Healey. Lambru dumped her body in the filtration plant and made it look like an escape." She shook her head. "I've got the proof, so I'm going to have to do something about him."

"No need," said Barray. "He got hurt in the plant at

the start of the lockdown. Tauceti is taking him to the military base tomorrow. I heard he's being transferred."

Kedron nodded when Calderosh looked at him questioningly. "He will not be coming back." In the level-five facility where Lambru was going, he'd be a nurse shark in a sea of krakens.

"Good." Calderosh looked at her beamer, as if she'd forgotten she had it. After a moment, she slipped it into her pocket.

Barray eyed Calderosh speculatively. "Do you have any contacts you trust in the shipping business?"

Kedron hoped his face didn't give away his disapproval about Barray negotiating with a woman who'd been willing to shoot them with a beamer.

"Maybe." She squinted one eye. "This is about that pet-trade shipment, right? I deal in grey-market data, but I have friends. I'd have to see what's being shipped."

"Is now a good time?" Barray's expression was the picture of innocence.

"Sure." Calderosh's tone held a wealth of skepticism.

Barray smiled. "Look to your left."

Boz decloaked, his skin and fur rippling as it changed shape and color. He sat only a few centimeters away from Calderosh's leg. He hissed.

Calderosh jumped right and banged into the entryway hard enough to rock the whole flitter.

Novo hissed from the right, then decloaked. She unfurled a bit of wing, then folded it again.

Calderosh froze. "What the hell are they?"

"Cats," said Barray.

"Right," said Calderosh sarcastically. "Because all cats have wings."

Barray laughed. "Only superior cats have wings."

BY THE END of the lockdown two hours later, Calderosh left the flitter after agreeing to use her contacts to ship the cats to Merganukhan a week after he arrived. His job was to sell the cats to Barray's supposed pet-trade contact, then split the profit with Barray and Calderosh. He'd pay for the shipping, so he'd have less incentive to steal the cargo for himself. He wasn't sure how that was supposed to work, but it satisfied Calderosh.

He disliked the idea that anyone believed he'd be involved in such a transaction, but realistically, after his last post, people would always question his motives. Regulations and ethics didn't always intersect.

Mindful of Calderosh's ubiquitous bots, he turned on the tech suppressor he'd confiscated from Lambru, then sat next to Barray on the bench. "Can we trust Calderosh?"

"I think so. She's got a good gig here, collecting and selling unrelated data. She's probably a finder of some sort, so she can sense what's valuable." Barray smiled. "I'll bet half the fund managers in the financial industry are unregistered minders. Finders for the research, forecasters for trends, filers to remember everything they hear or see. The CPS can't expose them without crashing the galactic economy." She snorted. "Or without admitting they've been ignoring the patterner class of minders for the last century, because there are too many of them."

"I never thought of it like that. Maybe that's why the Ayorinn Legacy meme is so persistent. The promise of freedom and equal treatment for minders would definitely resonate if it affects half the galactic population." He tapped his fingers on his thigh. "That would also explain why the CPS is so obsessed with obliterating it, and why they keep failing." He smiled wryly. "Not that they'd admit that, either."

Boz jumped onto the bench and butted Barray's arm, then licked her cheek.

She laughed and pushed him away. "Yes, you poor starving creature. I'll buy each of you an extra mealpack for lunch."

A distant attention tone sounded three times, followed by unintelligible words. Kedron's earwire told him it was the all-clear for returning to regular operation. The bongs that signaled the midday meal service would be coming soon.

"If I'm out of line, please tell me, but I want to pay for shipping and boarding the cats until you can come for them." What he really wanted was to pay off her restitution debt, but then they'd be right back where they were now. "You're taking the risks."

Her eyes narrowed in thought. "I'll split the cost with you. I'll give you codes for an account for my half. But I'm paying Calderosh's commission on the 'sale,' since it was my idea." She leaned forward and rested her elbows on her knees. "I'll resolve the restitution in ninety, maybe a hundred days. After that, I have to clean up the mess I left behind. You okay with waiting six months, or even longer?"

"Yes. Take as much time as you need." He tilted his head toward the cats, where Novo was grooming Boz. "They can stay here tonight, if they want."

The lunch bongs sounded.

Barray rubbed her neck and winced, then stood and stretched, exposing red and bruising skin underneath her tunic. "Maybe the medic will give me a painkiller."

Maybe he could accidentally drop Lambru on his head a couple of times on his way to the military base. He turned away before his expression gave him away.

He pushed to his feet. "I'll be giving my full contact information to the CRIO office. I'll make sure they know about the policy that requires them to let military indenturees send private communications to me until such time as my successor arrives."

She looked puzzled. "I don't remember reading that policy."

He scooped up the tech suppressor and put it in his pocket, then handed her tech bag to her.

"That's because I haven't written it yet."

She laughed and shook her head. "I think I'm a bad influence on you, Subcaptain Perfect."

He certainly hoped so.

EPILOGUE

As far as Ferra was concerned, the Merganukhan southern-continent spaceport was one of the best-kept secrets in the galaxy. Of all the transportation hubs she'd been to in her life, she'd never seen a more well-run facility.

Despite her attempt to keep herself iced, anticipation kept bubbling up and making her grin at the stupidest things, like the bright mid-afternoon summer sun streaming in through high, clerestory windows, or a small cleaning bot in the fresher.

Once her gravcart of luggage, her identification, and her person passed inspection, all she had to do was find the most handsome man on the planet. Fortunately, he'd pinged her with his location in the military section.

The easy part of her life after Tauceti left had been finishing her restitution. Lambru's sudden departure shattered his organization. After the cats left, she didn't have to worry about them being discovered. As a parting gift, they told her where Lambru had hidden his illegal chems laboratory. She told Calderosh, who got a company bonus for reporting it.

Ferra got bonuses for catching up on all the minor tech repairs. They went a lot faster when she could just rip out the surveillance tech instead of dancing around it. As a goodwill gesture, she made sure some of the better equipment ended up in Calderosh's parts lockers instead of the recycling bins.

The hard part had been going home. Her brother hadn't just sold her to pay his debts, he'd sold everything of hers he could get his hands on, including her flat and her flitter. He'd even gone to the trouble of declaring her dead for the insurance payout. It hadn't done him any good. He'd met with a very messy, very public fatal accident three weeks after she'd arrived at Argint d'Apa.

She spent five days in a luxury hotel, pampering herself while she tied up loose ends. Last time, she'd left in panic, only knowing what she didn't want. This time, she knew what she wanted and hoped for, and took the time to set things in motion for the next phase of her life.

Her stomach fluttered as she stepped into the space station's military lobby, suddenly worried that maybe Kedron couldn't make it, or had changed his mind. Exchanging dozens of messages and a couple of expensive realtime vid calls wasn't the same as seeing him in person.

Relief flooded her when she saw him striding purposefully toward her. His relaxed, confident smile made her grin like a fool, but she didn't care. He wore civilian clothes, but he still looked like a hero to her.

He waved his arm wide. "Welcome to Suck Flux, RSI."

She laughed. "I'm very glad to be here." She stepped in a little closer. "Would it be all right if I hugged you?"

He opened his arms. She wrapped him in a tight, fierce embrace, then let him go, or she'd never stop. He smelled good and felt better. She'd been dreaming of that and more for four months, eight days, and sixteen hours. Not that she had been running a countdown clock or anything.

He looked at the gravcart behind her. "Where's the rest of your stuff? I brought the biggest flitter in the transportation pool, just in case."

She shrugged. "That's it. I'll tell you about it tonight. We're still on for dinner?"

"Yeah, about that. All the good restaurants are booked, so I hope you don't mind eating at my place." He pointed toward an exit. "This way."

He offered to take her backpack, and she let him, even though the gravcart had room.

"You have a place?" She couldn't resist teasing him a little. He'd admitted to not having lived off base for his entire military career.

"Yeah, the base is short on command-level housing. I pointed out the policy that said base leadership shouldn't be clustered together, and volunteered for off-base quarters." The twinkle in his eye belied his serious expression.

She smiled. "It wouldn't happen to be a brand new policy, would it?"

He laughed, a sound she loved to hear. "No, it's an old policy, just not used very often."

His place turned out to be an isolated, ranch-style quick-formed house that backed up to a marshy eco-preserve. He'd chosen it because he'd kept the cats.

Her reunion with them was every bit as joyous as she'd imagined. Even reserved Novo was all over her, sending love and jumbled thoughts, and purring loud enough to wake the neighbors, if they'd had any. Boz tried to nuzzle inside her shirt like he was a kitten rather than a stealthy, lethal weapon of war.

"Did have trouble keeping Novo and Boz?" The Ground Division military manual she'd read during the interstellar flight to Merganukhan had been very adamant about not allowing personal pets in military quarters.

Kedron took off his boots and put them on the dry mat by the front door. "I couldn't find a boarding facility I trusted, so I rented a tiny apartment for them until I got approved for off-base housing." He twitched a smile as he brushed cat fur off his pant leg. "My coworkers assumed I was overnighting with a lover who has pets."

Ferra laughed. "You should have heard Calderosh complain about cat fur in Argint d'Apa's air ducts." Boz nuzzled her hair. "You'd like her, I think. The only reason she pulled that beamer on us in the flitter was because she thought we were working with Lambru. She's funny and surprisingly ethical. She only sells financial-related data, and won't deal in personal relationship information at all."

He sat cross-legged on the floor with her. "Dinner will be takeout from the base mess hall, but it's good." He pointed toward the front of the house, where the big military flitter sat waiting outside. "Why so little stuff?" He looked down at his splayed hand on his thigh. "Not staying?"

Nudging Boz away, she slid closer to Kedron. She slipped her hand into his. "I'm staying." She squeezed his hand gently, then waited until he met her gaze. "I really like you a lot. I've been dreaming about this day, but I want to take the time to do it right, at a pace that works for you. You're worth it."

He squeezed her hand. "I like you a lot, too. You and the cats are a good influence on me. I never lived with pets before, and now I can't imagine living without them. They remind me not to withdraw into my shell. You make me not want to."

His words touched her. "To answer your question, I don't have much stuff because I'm starting a new life." She explained what her brother had done.

With the love from the cats thrumming in her mind —and holding hands with the man she was falling for so fast she felt like she'd jumped off a cliff—she finally realized her brother had never loved her the way she'd loved him. *Move on, Barray.*

Novo crawled into her lap and curled up. "The financial industry is high risk for me. I don't ever want to be a target like that again. I liquidated all the accounts my brother couldn't find and left my old life for good. I'm keeping my new identity and starting a new career."

He stroked the back of her hand with his thumb. "In what?"

"Veterinary medicine. I'm studying for a basic vet med certification now and plan to sign on with a local clinic to get hands-on experience." She hoped to find someone who could help her learn to use her minder talent, too. She didn't want to keep it secret from Kedron, but first, she needed to research military policy on whether he'd have to report it if she told him.

"I'll ask around for recommendations, if you'd like." He smiled. "It's a good excuse to talk to people, instead of just issuing orders."

"Yes, please. I'd like to stay near the base. Near you, if you're alright with that. You make me feel safe." She looked around in the open living space, where the decor leaned heavily toward climbable sculpture and high padded shelves. "Can the cats stay here while I look for someplace to live?"

Kedron took in a deep breath and let it out quickly. "I'd kind of hoped you'd want to stay here. I haven't taken you on the tour yet, but the house is divided for two. There's a separate kitchen and—"

"Yes." She couldn't keep the joyous grin off her face. "I'll take it. I don't care how much you want in rent. I'll take it."

"I don't need the money. I need you." His vulnerable, serious look melted her heart.

"Could I kiss you?" she asked. "If it's too soon, just say—"

"Yes," he said.

He shared with her the sweetest kiss she'd ever had, with the promise of a bright future.

Novo rubbed her head contentedly on Ferra's arm. *You should mate with him. He is warm at night and good at petting.*

Ferra smiled. *Working on it.*

ABOUT THE BOOK

Thanks for reading *Cats of War*, and I hope you enjoyed meeting Ferra, Kedron, and the superior-in-every-way cats of war. If you want more space opera, adventure, and romance, check out OVERLOAD FLUX. Two misfits have secrets they must keep. But if they expose the secrets of a corrupt pharma corp, they may end up dead.

A shorter version of *Cats of War* debuted in the *Pets in Space 3* science fiction romance anthology. Profits from the Pets in Space® anthologies support Hero-Dogs.org, a charity that provides trained support dogs to disabled U.S. veterans and first-responders to improve their quality of life. I'd think cats of war would make fabulous support animals.

When the cure for a deadly disease is stolen, two misfits are all that stands between greed and intergalactic tragedy.

Luka Foxe can't let anyone know about his secret mental abilities. Debilitated by their influence when faced with violence, the brilliant forensic investigator now only takes assignments involving theft. But when he has to hunt down a hijacked vaccine for a galaxy-wide pandemic, the tragic first clue is his best friend's brutal murder.

Nightshift guard Mairwen Morganthur knows she must keep a low profile. The product of illegal genetic alteration, she's a lethal weapon with no social graces.

But when she's tasked to protect a detective with frightening intuition, she finds herself falling for him even though he could expose her.

Racing to recover the cure for a galaxy-wide pandemic, Luka is surprised by his developing feelings for the capable-but-mysterious guard. And Mairwen may have to risk everything by revealing her identity, with deadly mercenaries hot on their tail.

Can the unlikely pair survive an interplanetary conspiracy long enough to save lives and find love?

Overload Flux is the first novel in the sweeping Central Galactic Concordance space opera series. If you like haunted characters, compelling mysteries, and interstellar romance, then you'll enjoy Carol Van Natta's epic tale.

**Buy Overload Flux to uncover
cosmic corruption today!**

Author.CarolVanNatta.com/OF

*

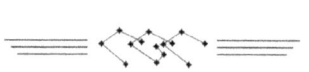

ABOUT THE AUTHOR

Carol Van Natta is a USA TODAY bestselling science fiction and fantasy author. Works include the award-winning Central Galactic Concordance space opera series and the Ice Age Shifters® paranormal romance series. In addition, she edits the Pets in Space science fiction romance anthology.

She shares her Colorado home with just the right number of eccentric cats. Connect with her on the web at Author.CarolVanNatta.com.